Bandit's Gold

When Joe Flint meets Matt Harper and Pete Brogan, he cannot help but be enticed by their tales of gold and mystery. They tell him of a legendary Mexican leader who reigned during the civil war, funding his leadership through a criminal network.

Drawn in by the promise of fortune, he follows his two new friends who are determined to find out the truth about the fort where the Mexican leader lived. But, along the way, they are attacked. Flint learns too late that he has put himself in the hands of madmen.

Will he find his fortune? Or has Flint got himself into a situation too dangerous to get out of alive?

By the same author

The Broken Trail

Bandit's Gold

Alex Frew

A Black Horse Western

ROBERT HALE · LONDON

© Alex Frew 2015
First published in Great Britain 2015

ISBN 978-0-7198-1681-9

Robert Hale Limited
Clerkenwell House
Clerkenwell Green
London EC1R 0HT

www.halebooks.com

Typeset by
Derek Doyle & Associates, Shaw Heath
Printed and bound in Great Britain by
CPI Antony Rowe, Chippenham and Eastbourne

CHAPTER 1

Joe Flint had gone across the territories looking for a way to make his fortune. He had been to many towns along the way: Deadwood and Tucson included. He had even taken jobs in the cattle business while he was looking for a way to make his mark. Once or twice men thought they could take advantage of his youth, when he went into bars looking for a drink or two and perhaps a game of cards. He knew faro and poker, but he also knew his limits and he would never be good enough to become a professional gambler. He was exceptionally sharp-eyed, though, noticing one night that a professional card-sharp tried to rig the hand. He had made short work of the man, getting him to hightail out of the place under threat of a bullet hole to the skull. Not wanting to splash his brains or challenge this youth, who had the dark fathomless eyes of an age-old sage, the gambler had wasted no time in getting out of town, feeling lucky to do so.

A tall man, older, than Flint and almost as lean, spoke to him after the game when the younger man was about to buy a drink with his fair share of the winnings. The man had a rangy look about him and dusty clothes, dark trousers that had once belonged to a good suit. He had a direct air and a kindly look to him, overlong dark hair that he swept back from the temples, and crinkles at the corners of his eyes that deepened when he smiled.

'You managed to put paid to his game.'

'Sure, thanks for that, stranger.'

'Name's Ty Landis. Haven't seen you around here before.'

'Didn't think you were a local.'

'I'm not. Rode out from Texas during the cattle season. Got a bit of wanderlust and ended up here in the territories. You?'

'Same kind of thing. I'm out and about doing jobs here and there. Probably get attached to one of the ranches in the end, but on the lookout for an opportunity to make some real money.'

'You mean by the sweat of your brow?' Ty gave him a long, lingering stare, as if the next few words would decide their acquaintanceship or not.

'Yep. When you have to commit crimes to live you're being stupid. A man can make his way without doing that kind of stuff.'

'Just the kind of thinking I like. You're young, though; you'll find life isn't as clear-cut as you think.'

They decided to look for work together after that. Landis told Flint his story: he had been married once, running livery in Deadwood. Things seemed to be going along well enough before he discovered that his young wife wasn't just entertaining him, but other men as well. She had gone off East with the richest of her suitors and was living well enough, last time he heard, in Denver.

For a while he had gone off the rails. This was two years down the line. Only now was he starting to get back his sense of humour and return to his old life.

'I figured I would just do this for a while – travel around

the territories and get some kind of measure over what I want to do with the rest of my days.'

'Maybe you should avenge yourself,' said Flint with the solemnity of a man who would have done so.

As for Flint, Landis found out little about his new companion, except that his first name was Joe and that he hailed from the Texas hill country. They searched around for their break, not knowing what their source of good fortune was going to be. When they encountered their fate it was so heavily disguised that they nearly passed up the opportunity. They were on the road to a little town called Pearson near the Sonoran desert, on the river, when they saw a whole lot of dust being stirred up in front of them.

They didn't have long to wait until the cause of the disturbance became plain to them. Two horses, both roans, were being ridden towards them. The horses pulled up and they saw two men. One of the men was about the same age as Flint but built in a much broader way, with long fair hair. The other was a big, solidly built older man. It was he who spoke to them.

'Help us out here. There's a posse after us and I swear it's for no crime you would recognize in a statute book.'

Flint was not the kind to hesitate.

'Get off your horses and undo your saddles real quick,' he said. 'Haul them over to the trees on the hills and hide there until there's an all-clear and just hope that you're telling the truth.'

The two men did as they were bidden, loosening straps with expert hands and dragging the saddles away, hiding in the cottonwood trees that grew on the slopes leading into town.

The horses might have been harder to hide, but Flint roped one and brought it to the back of his own mount while Landis followed suit and did the same with the other. Landis was following Flint's lead because he had been bored with the trail and the events of the day seemed to have taken an interesting turn.

As events turned out it was well for them that they had all moved so quickly. Another bigger flurry of dust on the dry trench that they called a road produced a mounted bunch of townspeople, seven in all, who stopped in front of Flint and his companion.

'You seen two reprobates coming this way?' asked the leader.

'No one passed me,' said Flint truthfully.

'Whose horses are those?' asked the leader suspiciously.

'Ours of course,' answered Flint agreeably. 'We had a string of six to get us through, these are the ones that're left.'

To the untrained eye one horse looks much like another and the person Flint was facing looked like some petty official who had barely put his backside on a saddle in his entire life.

'Anyways, what happened?' Flint asked.

'The crooks, swindlers, don't know how they did it, but that man fought seven bare-fist matches in two different saloons, for money and won 'em all. They must have been cheating some ways.'

'Come on, looks like they found the arroyo on the other side o' town and dry-gulched it out of here,' said another member of the posse.

The official gave a curt nod to the travellers and turned away with his men. They all rode off on their fruitless task. Flint waited until the dust settled down before he shouted the all-clear for the two men still hiding in the brushwood.

'Pete Brogan,' said the bigger man. 'This is my partner,

Matt Harper.'

'If they'd squared offta me Id've beaten them all,' said Matt, the expression on his face showing that he was entirely serious. Flint looked him over and saw a raw-boned brawny youth with shoulders that bunched up beneath his dusty brown coat. He believed him.

The travellers all rode away from the town, much to the regret of the two who had been heading there, and set up a camp together. They were soon telling tales around the fire that Flint had built out of brushwood, while sheltering under a rocky bluff in the hills.

'Matt here, he's quite a fighter,' said Pete. 'He's quick, strong and fearless.'

'Aw, shut it,' said the young man bashfully.

'The truth will out. Anyway I recognized his fighting stripes straight after we met. I'm tired of working for the cattlemen. The only way to make money is by taking a chance, so Matt here, he joins with me and I arrange bare-knuckle fights in different saloons around town. We bet a good purse that they can't beat him. A knockdown for a count of ten wins the match. Long story short—'

'I stormed it,' said Matt, but with an air of modesty. 'Pete's real good to me. He looks after the money an' every-thing.'

The others looked at Brogan, who shifted a little but put a brave face on the revelation.

'Look at it this way; the boy needs guidance. The money we earned is an investment. Anyway, word got round – as it would – of our prowess in the art of pugilism and the citi-zenry became antsy about the whole thing. Decided we were cheating in some way and chased us out of town. We were only too glad to go. Problem is, some of 'em decided they wanted their money back.'

The day was getting on so Flint cooked a turkey he had captured earlier. They sat afterwards drinking coffee he'd brewed over the fire.

'What exactly do you intend to do now?' asked Flint.

'Thinking of going back to the gold trade. Bit of a prospector,' said Brogan. He took a sip from the flask he kept in his breast pocket, without offering any to the others.

Landis looked at Flint. Brogan did not look like a prospector to them. They could see that Brogan had fastened on to a strong but simple-minded man like Matt just to make some money, as long as he didn't have to do any fighting of his own. Brogan took out a big cigar from another pocket.

Flint made a quick assessment of the man. He had met people like Brogan before, who were good at spinning fancies but who ended up making other people do as they wanted. He didn't like that kind because they usually ended up better off than the people they inveigled into doing their dirty work. Flint could bet that the money from the prize fights was still in his breast pocket in a fat leather wallet, and was money destined never to be shared with Harper, who had earned it in the first place.

'Sorry, gents. Only one I got.' He bit the end off the cigar, spat it out and lit up. Then he said something extraordinary. 'If I wanted I could join the rebel fort.'

'What rebel fort?' asked Flint.

'The one up in the hills near the south-west border, a few miles from Yuma. That's a laugh; town with a prison in it where they send the worst law-breakers, and not fifty miles away is a place teeming with them.'

'Sounds unlikely,' said Ty Landis. 'I've never heard of it.'

'You wouldn't,' said Brogan, 'Ramirez is a careful man. He keeps his rebels under control.'

'I think you're making it up,' said Flint. 'How would bandits get the resources to build an entire fort? The materials alone would cost a lot of money, and then they'd have to transport them to the hills. They'd come to the attention of the authorities right away.'

'That would be the case if it was the way it happened,' said Brogan. 'That's not the way it is. They're in an old fort from the days of the Civil War. Set up to keep an eye on the Mexican border. The Mexicans became real eager to lend a hand when there was conflict between the two parts of the States, if there was something in it for them.'

'But this fort,' interrupted Flint, sensing that Brogan could ramble on for hours if he was allowed to do so.

'I have connections there, is all I'm saying,' said Brogan. 'Ramirez – Juán is his first name, although he doesn't like anyone calling him that besides the dame he's hooked up with – will recruit any man who wants to help him in his cause.'

'What is his cause?'

'That I don't really know. But they say he's been accumulating enough gold and silver to finance whatever he wants to do, mostly from robberies spread out across the territories.'

'Sounds like a king.'

'He's a king all right, with his own kingdom. Now, gents, talking of robberies, I have a proposition for you.'

'What might that be?' asked Flint, sensing where the conversation was going.

'There's four of us now. I reckon we'll make a pretty good team, and we've got nothing to lose. What do you say we get together and relieve some of these here peasants of some ready cash? There's a whole lot of money in these silver-mining towns around this area. You, partner, look as if

11

you can handle a few oncomers with a weapon in your hands.' He was speaking directly to Landis. 'While you,' his focus shifted to Flint, 'why, you look as if you'd be like quicksilver getting out of there. Matt here can get in with his fists to get the money and do the close-up work, 'n I can plan the whole thing.'

Flint had set aside his gun while having his meal. Landis too had removed his gun belt so as to sit back against a large boulder in greater comfort, so they were effectively disarmed.

'We're not doing it,' said Flint evenly, putting his tin plate to one side.

'Letting the boy speak for you now?' sneered Brogan, looking slyly at Landis.

'No man speaks for me,' said Ty.

'You'll never amount to anything. Do you think you owe these townspeople a wooden dime? Trail riders are treated like dogs. They take you on when they want to and cast you off like dirt when they're finished with you. You deserve a little insurance. Isn't that right, Matt?'

'I s'pose so.' Matt was staring at the ground, his face red. It was obvious he was not happy with the proposal either, but was so dominated by the older man he did not know what to do.

'Well, it's an idea,' said Brogan. 'Sleep on it and we'll talk about the matter tomorrow.'

'I don't think so,' said Flint. 'In fact, we'll be parting company from you both as soon as we can. That's best, ain't it, Ty?' Landis nodded his agreement.

'Well, reckon I was foolish to let you in on my little scheme. Guess I misjudged you.' Brogan lumbered to his feet, his bulk looming large against the dark-blue sky. 'You'll do what you're told or I'll be obliged to leave no evidence.'

Flint was already facing him, but his gun was yards away. Landis was still sitting down and he was still unarmed, too. Brogan looked like the kind of man who could drill two sitting targets straight through the heart without any trouble.

'Settle down,' said Flint. 'We don't want this.'

'Too late,' said Brogan, and laughed out loud. It was a wild, almost hysterical laugh and Flint knew at once that the man was mad, probably had been for a while, his brain curdled by drink and lord knows what diseases he had picked up from the whores used in various towns. Brogan raised his twin Colts, forefingers tightening on the triggers. Behind where he stood, Flint could hear Ty scrambling to his feet. They would both be dead in seconds.

Flint did not seem to move, but Brogan gave a grunt more of surprise than pain. He looked down to see the handle of the knife that seemed to grow from his chest. There was only a thin trickle of blood below the blade as it severed the arteries that carried the lifeblood from his heart to his brain. Brogan gave a thin, choking sound and fell face forward into the fire, already dead.

His hair began to burn. There was a smell of cooking flesh.

'Give me a hand,' said Flint curtly. The other two helped him move the body and beat the fire out of his hair; the face had already melted beyond all recognition. Flint recovered his blade, wiping it clean on the man's jacket.

'We'll get rid of him fast,' he said.

CHAPTER TWO

Nearly two weeks after the death of Pete Brogan the three men made their way across a chain of hills, each seemingly steeper than the last, until they found they were looking out at the plains again. Matt was still silent, brooding, having thrown his lot in with the other two because he really had no choice.

Just after the death of Brogan – which wasn't an ice-cold killing no matter how you looked at it – Matt had launched his solid body at Flint and sent him reeling with a couple of pounding blows that would have knocked out a lesser man. Flint, no mean adversary in the fist area, had punched back, but he had been driven down the slope, and would have been defeated by a man who was obviously as good at using his fists as Brogan had boasted; perhaps he would have even been punched to death by his opponent. But there was a dry clicking sound behind Harper and an equally dry voice spoke to him.

'Stop right now or the back of your head'll vanish, son.' Matt stopped his battering, joined them resentfully, and helped them to get rid of the body, which they covered in rocks, being unable to dig a grave.

He had joined them after promising that he would not attack either of them again. For the first few days he seemed to be sullen and angry all the time, then his naturally cheerful nature reasserted itself and he was a good and willing companion, accepting that he was better off with people

14

than without them. Sometimes Landis would notice that Matt would glare at Flint when he thought the latter was not observing him, and he realized that the resentment over the loss of the man Matt had thought was his friend was not over.

They had come on a long trip heading towards the border with Mexico because Flint, who seemed to have an unerring sense of direction, was leading them to some target that only he seemed to know about. The other two were content to follow; Landis because he had faith in the younger man and Matt because he had nowhere else to go.

Now they were looking out at an adobe ranch on the plain. It was cooler and greener on this side of the territory; they could see the grass and trees surrounding the compact white building. Out back there was a corral, which contained a few horses. Other horses, four in all, were hitched in front of the gates of the ranch. A solid wall had been built in front of the ranch, so the only way to see what was going on was through the open gates.

'We need supplies, and we don't have much money,' said Flint. 'We'll see what we can do for the owner, then get on our way.'

'Why do we need to do anything in exchange?' asked Matt.

'What?'

'Brogan would've looked after the three of us. Doesn't seem that hard to go in there and get what we want.'

'Matt, you ever learned the concept of right and wrong?' inquired Landis.

'Never had no schooling. Everyone takes what they want, why shouldn't we?'

'Because that's just the way it is,' said Flint. 'We'll go in real easy, offer our services – there's always something needing done on a ranch – then be on our way.'

'OK, you get your way as usual.' Matt slipped off his horse.

'What do you mean by that?' Flint was already standing.

'You know full well Brogan would've bested you if you hadn't cheated by using a knife.'

'Your friend was going to kill me.'

'Gee, he was fulla wind and piss, bluster too. He just wanted you to do a few things that would've made us all wealthier.'

For a moment it looked as if Matt was going to attack Flint again. Flint stood very still. He was armed now. They had given the other young man a chance, but if he wanted to bring matters to a head right now that was his choice.

'Matt, we'll cut you adrift right now,' said Landis. 'You have a choice in the matter you've just raised: you can settle this either way or cut and run.'

'He's right,' said Flint. 'I didn't want to kill your partner but it sure looked as if he was going to use those firing irons.'

'Do you mean that?' Harper looked full into Flint's face.

'I do.'

For a moment it seemed as if Matt was about to rebel and ride away, then some kind of calculation took place beneath that thatch of fair hair.

'Then I guess I'll have to go with that. Friends?' He held out a big bony hand.

'Sure.' Flint shook him by the hand. The tension seemed to drain from the air. 'Now let's go here and do things right.'

Distances can be deceptive on the plain and it took them another ten minutes to get close to the ranch. The horses tied up were a varied bunch, a pinto, a roan, a grey and even a big gelding. This worried Flint, since the horses in a ranch were usually of one type or another. As they came closer he could hear some high-pitched female cries.

'Help! Help!' They sounded like the voice of one in despair.

'Ty, you stay here and guard the place,' said Flint, drawing out his Colt .44. 'You, Matt, get ready to come in when I give you a shout.'

'I'm coming in right now.' There was nothing wrong with his courage, at least.

'Don't be stupid. If I can get in there it's just one target. I might need you to back me up. Now get to the side of those gates.' Without waiting to see if his orders were being obeyed Flint spurred his horse forward, thundered through the gates of the ranch and into the yard.

There a horrific sight met his eyes. The four raiders had been busy. Two men who were obviously workers of the peon class lay dead on the ground, one of them shot through the head, the other riddled through the body with bullets. Three men wearing the striped shirts and black trousers of bandits were forcing a young girl over a large water barrel in the yard. It was obvious they were going to take her, for her skirts had already been pulled up, with the intention that they were going to take turns with her. Even as he watched, the man who had her in his grasp, who was tall, with a long, flowing moustache, slapped her across the face to stop her beating at him with frantic hands.

'Stop it, bitch,' he said, 'I've killed men for less.'

Flint took in the situation at once, riding into the yard, flinging himself off the back of his horse and sheltering behind an unhitched buckboard yards from where the proposed act was taking place. The breath was jarred out of his body and for a second he was a sitting target while he tried

17

to recover from his rapid descent. Two of the men immediately abandoned the girl and went to deal with the intruder, obviously thinking that he was another of the hands who had come back from his work and had discovered them in their work. They were grinning all over their broad faces, coming towards the wagon with the obvious intention of finishing him off.

Flint rolled away from where he had landed and jumped up at the tail of the wagon, which sat at an angle, tilted forward on its axles. This meant that the two men were side-on to where he was standing. He took the opportunity and put a bullet in the nearest one, a man almost as tall as the one who was still with the girl. The bullet caught this individual on the shoulder and the man whirled away as if he had been punched with a giant fist. He gave vent to a few choice curses that had not been learned at his mother's knee.

The far away individual was smaller than the first, with far better reactions. He ran round the buckboard and would have been able to shoot Flint in the back if it hadn't been for the fact that Flint had already thought of this and had retreated swiftly. The smaller man came back round and was met by a bullet that took him in the throat. There was a great spurt of blood as the bullet emerged from the back of his neck. The man put both his hands to his throat as if to stem the flow that rushed out of the hole made by the bullet. This was to be his last act on earth, because he could not stem the tide that rushed out of the hole. He fell to his face, his hat tumbling over and over until it came to rest at Flint's feet. This all happened in the space of a few seconds.

The man who had been paying his attentions to the girl gave a savage curse. He sprang away from his victim and ran to the other side of the yard, pulling out a long-barrelled gun as he did so. Flint recognized the danger right away. The man had not tried to push the girl in front as a human shield because he did not have enough time to do so. He had realized that he would have been shot down like the dog he was.

For the first time Flint could see that he was in real trouble. This one was evidently the leader of the group, knowing full well how to handle the action around him. This was a rare breed, someone who could remain calm and focus on his target in the midst of action. Flint took the most sensible course of action and dived behind the buckboard as the man raised his gun and fired. Three shots thudded rapidly into the wood where, a second earlier, his head had been.

He raised his own weapon and fired once, then again, but there was an empty click and he realized that he had run out of bullets. Flint had a couple of choices now; he could try and get to one of the dead men and filch his gun, or he could use his silent, lethal friend. He leapt up, at the same time grabbing at his knife, only to realize it was not there. A bolt of horror shot through him as he saw it lying yards away, beside the man he had shot in the throat. It must have fallen out when he was moving around.

Flint was unarmed. He took the only course of action possible and dived towards his knife. There was a roar of triumph from the tall guy and he felt a bullet pass so close to his head that he could feel a hot flush on the side of his face where the bullet had just missed tearing off his jaw.

He felt the handle of the knife in his hand even as his right shoulder jarred against the ground. This time a bullet tore through the fabric of his jeans on the upper thigh, burning across the flesh of his leg. Any closer and he would have been crippled for life.

Flint gave a wild scream of pure hatred, trusted to his instincts and threw the knife, which arced straight and true through the air. At the same time he rolled over and over on the soil until he was almost at the feet of the girl. There was a strange silence, then a distinct gurgling sound like someone trying to be sick. He stood and turned to see that the tall gunman had the knife embedded in his left eye. The gunman dropped his weapon and clawed ineffectually at his own face, then dropped to the ground, twitched and lay still.

Flint stood up and faced the girl. She backed away from him, a look of terror on her attractive features. He tried to look at the situation from her point of view.

'Don't harm me,' she said.

'It's all right.' He held up both hands. 'Look, I'm unarmed.'

Her eyes were still wide with fear, but now she was looking over his shoulder. He whirled around to see a fourth man, who had obviously been raiding the ranch, bursting out of the building. The fourth raider was wearing dark clothes, had long flowing hair and was screaming in a mixture of English and Spanish as he ran towards Flint, holding a short cavalry sword that had once seen better days.

'*El Diablo*! Murdering bastard! You are dead!'

Since Flint was now unarmed it looked as if the blade was going to penetrate his heart – and in the brief second he had left he was sure the girl would follow soon after.

Then a demon whirlwind entered the fray. Harper, moving at a speed he had never displayed before, came running into the open area and grabbed the man by the hair, jerking him backwards. The man turned, screaming obscenities at the new arrival and slashed out with his sword. But Matt ducked under the wild swings the man took at him and pounded forwards with his fists. He made contact with the man four, five six, seven times, until there was an unconscious, barely breathing, bloody heap of flesh and bone at his feet. Then the man gave a sigh, expiring where he lay, his breathing cut off by the dust.

By this time Ty Landis had also arrived on the scene. He looked at the bodies around without too much concern now that he knew Flint was OK.

Flint still stood beside the girl. Accompanied by Harper, Landis came over to his travelling companion.

'Looks like you did a thorough job on this lot,' he said.

The girl was soon persuaded that the new arrivals were not going to harm her in any way. In fact she was even more reassured when they helped her get rid of the bodies by the simple expedient of taking them to the nearest hole – not hard to find in this landscape, dropping them in, then covering them in debris.

They returned to find the girl inside the building. She was making food and coffee for them, but more to steady her nerves after the carnage she had witnessed than for their benefit. While they sat at the big kitchen table she told them about her circumstances. Flint could not help noticing that she was a remarkably pretty girl, with high cheekbones and very dark eyes.

'My name is Morven Drake,' she explained. 'I live here with my father and our workers. My mother died a few years ago of a fever. Father set off early because he was taking some horses into the nearest town. He warned us to be on our guard because our ranch is so remote, but when the men came here they seemed so reasonable, wanted to buy some stock. Those poor workers.' For a moment her eyes were bright with unshed tears. It was obvious that she did not want to break down in front of her rescuers.

'But who are they at all?' asked Flint.

'They are raiders from the hills,' said the girl. 'That's who I think they are.'

'What do you mean, raiders?' pressed Flint.

'Bandits. I think they are bandits. I've heard ... rumours.'

'Like what?'

'That there's a whole lot of them up there. The authorities are turning a blind eye at the moment. But I've also heard they have a leader.'

'What's his name?'

'I don't really know.' The girl had a look of despair on her face. 'I just think it isn't safe here any more, and that's strange.'

'Why is it strange?'

'Because I've heard that they want to leave the locals alone, the towns and the ranches. They're after other kinds of wealth in different areas.'

On the face of it her assertions did not make sense. After all, a band of robbers was a band of robbers; they would just take what they wanted when they wanted it. But deeper thought showed that if they wanted to keep their hideout secure it made sense for them to leave the locals alone. The hills were in an area known as the Devil's Highway, between the territories and the border, which had been inhabited by ancient Indian tribes. They had over fifty square miles of territory with wooded thickets on either side leading up to the hills. That meant they were fairly secure as long as the three towns along the tributary of the Colorado River and the ranchers did not band together to get them out.

'I think I know what's happening,' said Landis. 'They're entrenched in their fort. The country over here is rocky, meaning that it's not a great place for the herders to leave their cattle. It's hard to get here. Of course they're not going to hack off the people near them. It's so they blend in with their surroundings and get left alone by the locals.'

'That doesn't explain why they attacked me,' said the girl, the tears now threatening to spill over on to her smooth cheeks.

'The explanation is quite easy.' said Flint. 'They are criminals, after all. The one who was trying to hurt you when I arrived was stinking of booze, and it looks to me as if he was the leader. I think he just decided he wanted to take something or someone for himself in defiance of orders.' Flint rubbed his jaw thoughtfully. 'This puts a different spin on things. I think that if that bunch weren't lying dead out there they might well have been killed by their own kind.'

'What do you mean?'

'Just what I said: their leader obviously wants to keep his distance from locals.'

'I don't care. I want to get out of here for good. My father has relatives in Tucson. When he gets back I'm going to tell him I'm leaving.'

'I don't think you should,' said Flint slowly. 'You're safer than you realize.'

'We'll see,' said the girl, rising up as she heard the clatter of hoofs at the gates. 'That's my father.' She seemed to have recovered her composure a little.

Flint looked cynically at the other two.

'At least we'll get a job,' he said.

CHAPTER THREE

Hadfield Drake, Morven's father, turned out to be a grey-haired rancher, looking much older than his fifty-something years. He wore an air of undefined sadness, and it was clear that he was still missing his wife. Although he was grateful to Flint for saving his daughter, he was saddened to learn about the death of those he had employed.

'They were good, hard-working boys,' he said. 'I'll get them a decent Christian burial and let their families know.'

He managed to persuade Morven to stay until they had more money in the bank, then they could think about selling up and going to town.

When he learned that the three men who had rescued his daughter were looking for work he took them on at once, because he needed some of his cattle to be driven to market in Milton, the biggest of the three towns. Then he needed some hands to round up and drive his other stock to the meadows on the southern uplands to help them get fat for the winter.

Landis and Flint took the jobs at once, although Flint sensed some hesitation in Harper. They were given berths in the bunkhouse that belonged to the ranch, sharing it with some of the other men employed there. Mainly Mexican, the other hands seemed to have a fatalistic view about what had happened to their friends, which puzzled Flint. If his companions had been killed he would have gone in with all guns blazing for revenge. Perhaps that was not their culture, or maybe they were afraid of rousing the wrath of the criminals and bringing their full might down upon them.

One night, when they were out back of the ranch sitting around the campfire, just the three of them, Harper expressed his dissatisfaction with the way things had turned out.

'I just want an end to all this.'

'An end to what?'

'All this trailin' around. Maybe you could do me a favour, Landis?'

'Like what, Matt?'

'Maybe you could be my manager, like Brogan: get me out of this. I was made to use my fists. We could go into the town and get some action.'

'Uh huh.' Landis rolled a cigarette with the makings he always kept in a drawstring bag. He deliberately kept Harper waiting as he blew a plume of smoke into the sparks shooting up from the dry brushwood fire. 'And why would I want to do that?'

'Because you would get a big share of the purse, that's why, and because I have no way with words to talk to them big shots—'

'What big shots?' interrupted Flint. 'Do you think these towns have regular bouts?'

'I ain't the only one who fights,' said Harper, glaring at Flint.

'Sure, I know, but you won't last long at that game.'

'I'll last long enough to collect quite a few winnings.'

'What, dragging from town to town until you meet your match, spending your winnings at seedy hotels on women and drink? Then what?'

'I guess I don't know,' mumbled Matt. 'At least I got

some plan.'

'Flint's right,' said Landis. 'You'd encounter some mean idiots like you did in Pearson who didn't want you to get your rightful winnings. There's certain games where they don't like someone who's really good.'

'Well, if you don't want to manage me, I'll be off and find someone who can.'

'I have an idea,' said Flint. 'Been thinking about it for a while.'

'Better be a good one,' said Harper, 'because I'm out of here if it ain't, next three days maximum.'

'I say we go after the gold Brogan was talking about,' said Flint.

'What? That's a crazy idea,' said Harper.

'Why would you think that was even possible?' For the first time since they had met Landis looked at Flint as if he doubted the other man's sanity. 'Brogan was full of horse-shit. He was making it all up.'

'Well, Matt, you knew Brogan quite well. Was he a brag-gart who didn't know a thing or was he telling the truth? He gave me the impression he couldn't have arranged a shindig in a brothel.'

Matt looked a little uncomfortable.

'Well, we turned to the prizefighting again after what happened in Lemmon's Creek. Guess I'm still a wanted man in that area.'

'What happened?'

'Well, truth is we needed money, so he got me to do a robbery in a store; easier than a bank, he said. They seen my face and they had reports of us getting out of there. Didn't get away with all that much, either.'

'So it's beginning to look as if Brogan was using a man who was a simpleton – no offence intended, pal – to carry out a bunch of petty crimes. So he really was full of horse-shit,' said Landis. 'I guess that makes him an unreliable source.'

'You would think so,' said Flint slowly. 'Did he ever talk to you of the robbers in these hills?'

'He did that, but he was afraid of them, deadly afraid.'

'Why was that?'

Harper looked at the ground as one who was being faced with an unpleasant thought. Now he lifted his head and looked at their faces as one who had finally decided to tell the truth.

'God rest him! I liked the big man, but he was a coward, he did the robbin' through me and only challenged when he thought he had the upper hand, like he did with you and Landis. He was trying to bully you into doing what he wanted.'

He looked at them earnestly and suddenly Flint knew that this was a man who was lost on his own, who needed a hand to guide him, that despite the power in his fists he was like a child inside.

'He seemed to know a lot about them robbers, I don't know how, but he was always talking about how much gold they had, all hidden up there if a man could get to it. I swear he thought it was true, that's all I can say.'

'Then we're going to do what we should have done a while ago,' said Flint.

'What's that?' asked Landis.

'We're going to secure our future.'

When they went to see Drake three days later he was sorry that they were going to leave, but already resigned.

'I know the drive is over for now, but if you boys want to stay on I'll give you a living wage and make you useful about the place.'

'Thanks,' said Flint, who had made the approach, 'but we're moving on.' He had already spent some of their hard-earned money on a cache of weapons and ammunition that they had hidden up in the hills. Landis was a bit worried by this, but he had a policy that one man should lead and the others should follow. Any other way invited arguments. You just had to follow the right man. Besides, he trusted Flint in a way that he had never trusted any other man. If Flint wanted things to be this way Landis was not going to oppose him.

'You're going?' said the girl, who chanced upon them all standing there as she came out of the ranch. For the first time Flint felt uncomfortable about his decision. He did not see much of her from day to day but now he realized that she was probably the one reason he had stayed so long.

'We'll be back,' he told her. 'Just got other things to do.'

'We're much safer with you around,' she said. She looked at all three of them, but they knew she meant one person in particular.

'That's good to know, but I told you, that was just drunk idiots. There's been no reprisals, have there, even though they're gone?'

'No, that's true.' The girl stepped closer to him. 'It's just that things feel better when the three of you are around.'

'I guess.' Flint tried to sound indifferent, but his heart was beating so fast and so loudly he feared it might burst out of his chest. It was an effort for him to feign indifference when a girl with deep, dark eyes and plump, slightly parted lips was looking at him that way. 'We'll be around, as I say. You have your own men, and your pa says he is going to recruit others real soon, ma'am.' He tipped his hat to her and mounted his steed.

As they rode away from the ranch he looked back. She was still standing there, watching them go. Suddenly he had a reason for making this a successful mission.

'She sure has taken a shine to you,' said Landis after they had been riding for ten minutes or so.

'Could be,' said Flint, still pretending indifference. 'Let's concentrate on this. You boys know what to do?'

'I've half a mind to turn and go,' said Harper.

'Half a mind is all you got,' said Landis cheerfully.

'Them's fightin' words.'

'Well, keep them fists of yours for whoever we're about to face.'

They rode steadily onwards. The hills became steeper as they went and the thickets on either side of them deepened as they progressed, forcing them to go forward on the one already beaten trail. They seemed to ride forever upwards and Flint realized that part of the reason why the band of criminals had been so successful in the past was the fact it was so difficult to get to them in the first place. The other reason was that the thickets, made up of low bushes, iron-wood trees and pines, were the best hiding-place for anyone. You could have hidden ten thousand men in there and no one would know they were present. The one trail made it easy for those who commanded these hills to look out for intruders.

They had discussed their strategy while out on the plains, keeping their voices low because sound carried great distances in that kind of terrain.

'We'll tell them that we want to join them because we're wanted men,' said Flint. 'We use the circumstances Matt told us about to get in with them.'

'They might have heard about it,' said Harper.

'I doubt it, pal; these guys are serious. They don't take

details of every piddling hold-up. Once we're in with them we find out where they store the gold, get as much as we can – once we spot an opportunity to do so – then we get out of there.'

'Sure seems like a risky thing to do,' said Ty, blowing plumes of smoke from both nostrils, a trick he had when concentrating.

'There's an old saying that says something about pain and gain,' said Flint. 'The point is, we stay together as much as we can and that lets us get in there to do what we have to do. Just do as I say.'

'Seems a bit illegal,' said Landis.

'We'll be taking whatever treasure we can find,' said Flint. 'These are robbers, we're not holding up the First National bank. We'll redistribute the money, that way we make it up to society. The difficult thing'll be getting away. Once we do that we'll be pretty much set up to do what we want.'

He had made his point well. Now, as they rode together up the trail, the three of them strung out with Flint in the lead so that they presented a wider target, the trail widened and became rockier. Even though he had never been here before Flint knew that this was because certain plants and trees could not grow above a certain height because they weren't getting enough nutrient from the bare soil at the top of the hills. The thickets of trees had given way to low, scrubby vegetation, while the hills dipped and rolled in all directions, cutting off a clear view of where they were heading.

It was quiet up here in the mountains, so it was easy for them to hear the click of weapons cocked. Three men stepped out of a rocky recess, all wearing the broad-brimmed hats of the bandit, with bullet belts criss-crossed over their chests. All three carried twin six-shooters. The man at the front, who was larger than the other two, lifted his head. Flint felt a thrill of superstitious fear, as he looked the man full in the face.

It was Brogan, large as life and twice as evil.

'Kill them!' barked Brogan.

CHAPTER FOUR

Luckily Flint was able to keep a cool head as he looked at the men who were about to kill them. He had two reasons for this coolness, one being that it had been a long hard ride and it was hard to get worked up even when you were facing mortal danger. The other was that he had the confidence of youth, allied with a sense that the men beside Brogan were too slow in responding to his command. He had a sense that this was a bluff on the part of the big man to try and establish some kind of dominance over the new arrivals. Brogan was waiting to see how they would respond.

'Wait!' Flint squared up to the bandits and their leader. 'We're here because we can help you.'

'Hold your fire,' said Brogan in a low voice to the men beside him. Certainly there was no thought that they were going to put their weapons away. They kept them levelled firmly on the three men in front of them. Flint knew enough to understand that he had to put his case as quickly and as firmly as possible.

'We're here to join you. We can work for you.'

'Do these two have tongues?' asked Brogan.

'I don't know what to say,' said Matt. Flint detected a slight tremor in his voice and gave an inward curse. Harper could very well let some superstitious terror undo him, thinking this was a ghost of some kind.

'I speak,' said Ty Landis, 'Just thought I'd give it one singer one song.'

Brogan took off his hat and scratched at his short-haired pate. Although long hair was quite common around these parts a lot of men chose to have it short because it took away some of the heat from their heads, a heat which in this climate could be considerable. When he did this it immediately became clear that he was younger than the man Flint had killed, with a leaner face. Obviously he was the younger brother of the dead man, but with a look of intelligence and poise about him that the other Brogan had not possessed.

'So you're going to help us,' said Brogan. 'What about the fact that you might be government agents sent here to do a bit of weeding out? You considered that angle?'

'We're not government agents,' said Flint. 'Matter of fact we're the very opposite. I got together with these boys here and we raided a few banks and stores in the likes of Tucson and Pearson. We've been hiding out in a ranching station for the last few weeks.'

Except for the criminal part this was more or less true. Flint had a steely glare that defied the other man's gaze, so that Brogan looked away to his companions.

'What do you think, boys?'

'They looks fit,' said the older of the two men, 'we can always use labour.' He shrugged, having passed enough comment.

'We kill them and let their corpses feed the buzzards,' said the other man.

The long journey and the heat had taken something out of the three of them. For the first time Flint was aware that his boldness in coming here might be very flawed indeed. In the back of his mind there was a thought about this younger brother. He did not yet know what kind of relationship the two Brogans had had with each other. If they had held nothing but hatred – which was quite common in brothers in this part of the world – then the killing wouldn't matter because the subject would not come up. If the pair of them had been fond of each other or had had some kind of regard then it would be harder to deal with the situation, because if it came out that Flint had knifed the elder brother in the heart the younger version would not take this too well. This, of course was an understatement. He would want revenge on his brother's killer.

'OK. Let's say who we are. I'm Shaun Brogan. These are two of my men, Jimez and Raul. We kill interlopers.' He said this with a wolfish grin that showed he thought he was being funny.

'I'm Joe Flint, these are—'

'Let the men speak for themselves!' thundered Brogan.

'Ty Landis.'

'Matt Harper.'

They had toyed with the idea of giving false names but quickly decided against this. Harper was clearly not into pretending to be someone else and would reveal his true identity quite quickly, while it was quite easy for either Ty or Joe to slip up by not responding in the right way when someone spoke to them, risking instant death from people who tended to have hair-trigger tempers.

'Easy enough to remember,' grunted Brogan. He narrowed his eyes as he looked at Matt. 'What's wrong with you, buck?'

'Nothing,' said Matt sullenly. If the question had been directed at Flint he, Flint, would have immediately changed the subject, but Matt, red in the face and not just from the sun, lowered his head.

'You got problems?'

'He's just tired,' said Flint. 'We all are. We thought we might have been there by now. We want to meet Ramirez.'

Flint was glad he had taken the lead in the conversation. His biggest fear was that if Matt was needled enough he would blurt out his knowledge of the older Brogan.

'Ramirez? You know the name? How could that be the case?'

Brogan raised his guns and so did the other two. Flint decided quickly that he had to take a sardonic approach because this was the humour to which these kinds of men could relate.

'Everyone who has been around this part of the world knows the mighty Ramirez. He's a big shot, el gran jefe in these parts. They don't mention his name out loud much in the three towns of the Devil's Trail – but you hear rumours. Then his name is whispered in dark corners and you begin to wonder what kind of man this is who can inspire so much awe.'

The three towns of which he spoke were Milton, Newmains and Desert Hills, all linked by being border towns on the banks of the same tributary of the Colorado river. They were apart but shared trade links, families and officials as a protection against the frequent raids from across the divide. They might have been seen as easy pickings by bands of robbers – indeed would have been if

Ramirez hadn't been so far-sighted, realizing that it is a lot harder to hide out in the open if you are raiding settlement towns. His men went into these when they wanted supplies they just couldn't get up here in the hills, like new skillets or spices for their favourite meals, but otherwise they left the townspeople alone.

That is not to say that from time to time there wasn't any grumbling among the storekeepers and tradesmen about dealing with criminals, but they were always polite, paid in cash and left the townspeople alone. There was a general feeling that you treated the bandits like you would a hornet's nest. If it was too close to home you would set it alight, flush out the inhabitants and destroy them for the pests that they were. If it was far enough away you left well alone. Flint had learned these facts from Hadfield Drake when he was conversing with the older man back at the ranch.

'Very good,' said Shaun Brogan, referring to the name being whispered in dark corners. 'Sure have a feeling that despite your tender years you're the leader of the three. Yep, we'll take you to meet our esteemed leader. It seems you've had a stay of execution – for now. Wait where you are, boys, 'til I prepare you for the trip.'

As he said these words he nodded to his companions and once more their weapons were levelled at the three strangers. The point they had reached on this part of the trail was at a natural pass, where a large boulder blocked the way causing the trail to meander around the back of the huge sand-coloured rock that was nearly three times the height of Shaun Brogan. It was round the back of this, invisible to prying eyes, that the bandits had hidden their horses – and other things besides. Brogan came back carrying three iron shackles and lengths of grey cloth. It was immediately obvious what he was going to do. This did not go down too well with Matt Harper or Landis. Ty shied his horse at an angle from Flint.

'What in blue heaven…? Ya expect to do this to us? Come on, Flint, we've had enough of this monkeying.'

Harper said nothing, but lowered his head, red spots rising on his high cheekbones, fists clenching on his horse's reins.

' 'Fraid it's too late for that, men.' Brogan threw the shackles at the feet of his men and pulled out twin guns with ebony grips, pointing them firmly at the intruders. 'Just dismount boys. We'll get you back up again.'

Only Flint remained calm, the other two getting off their horses' backs with a look that boded physical rebellion. The two Mexicans put down their weapons, picked up the shackles and made towards the three men. One grabbed Matt Harper, who immediately reacted with his fighting instincts. Such was the force of the blow that the man actually flew backwards several feet before landing with an audible thud on the dusty ground.

Harper immediately found two weapons pointed at him – and one of them belonged to Flint. He looked wordlessly from Brogan to the man who had promised them such riches that they would never have to work again.

'Now listen, Matt, Ty, these men have got a job to do; let them get on with it or they'll carry out their original threat and I for one don't want to end up being a fancy meal for some bobcat and a bunch of vultures.'

'Well, well.' Brogan looked mildly astonished that he was being backed up by one of the very intruders he was attempting to deal with.

Harper breathed deeply and stood with his hands at his sides, while Ty took his hands away from his guns. In the meantime Flint put his gun away and slid off his horse, showing solidarity with the other two.

'Drop your gunbelts,' said Brogan. Flint did so, facing the man, knowing that this was a crucial moment for Ty, who was a gunman with all his soul and would look upon divesting his person of weapons the way someone else might look on losing a child. Flint's expression did not change as he spoke the words that might very well stop Ty from gunning down those who might lead them to prosperity.

'We'll get them back, right?'

'We'll think about it; chances are sure high, we just got to take a few precautions is all.' From the corner of his eye Flint saw Ty relax a little.

The shackles were fastened around Flint's legs by Jimez, who seemed to have done this before, so efficient was he at the task. Flint would have appreciated a clothes'-peg on his nose during the process, because it was evident that whatever else he believed in, the man was not too good at applying soap and water. When he tied the blindfold on after fastening the leg-irons the blast of his spicy breath made Flint's eyes water. He heard the other two behind him receiving the same kind of treatment. The blindfold was made from an old blanket, with a variety of nameless scents. Flint was glad he had not eaten heavily before going on this mission. He could see nothing through the thick material but his eyes soon began to adjust and see fragments of light around the periphery of his blindfold.

The worst part of the experience was the last. Brogan put down his gun and came to help his men. Flint had imagined they would sit sideways on their horses rather like the ladies in town who rode to church on Sunday, with their hands on the reins so they would at least have some control. Instead he was picked up by several pairs of rough hands and thrown face forward across the saddle, the raised leather at the edges pressing into his arms. From the cries of protest behind him he could detect that the other two were not being as stoic about the matter as he was.

He hoped that they would be able to use reason to work out what was happening to them. That they had been taken captive in this way was a good sign. The criminals had obviously brought other men to their encampment in the same manner. Flint presumed that if a man could persuade the leader he was fit to stay this would be the end of the recruitment process.

The horses were put in a line and, obedient as horses are, although a little perturbed by the way they were carrying their burdens, the animals moved along at a shouted word from Raul, who led them, accompanying him, in a string. Flint could feel the breath being driven out of his chest each time they pounded down into a hollow, then for a few minutes he felt his body slide back as they climbed another steep hill. Behind him he could hear Matt, no stoic he, giving forth a steady stream of curses in a guttural voice that did not augur well for those who had put him in this position should he ever be able to take his revenge.

It was hard to tell the time when you were in this position, but Flint estimated that half an hour had passed before the horses were brought to a clip-clopping halt. Brogan gave a gruff order and their burdens were pulled down from their saddles, falling to the ground like sacks of potatoes, just as they had been carried. None too gentle hands hauled them to their feet, while those same hands removed their blindfolds.

'Get your stinking paws off me,' said Harper.

'I sure share that sentiment,' said Ty.

'Shut up the pair of you,' said Flint, but keeping his voice light. 'Look at this.'

In his mind he had pictured the fort as no more than an earth fortification like the ones he had seen in the desert; either that or something that had been fenced in by the army all those years ago when they were up here. Instead he discovered that Fort Lincoln was huge. The whole thing had been constructed on a natural plateau in between the rolling hills – indeed some of the land may have been artificially flattened for that very purpose. The walls were made from a mixture of adobe and stones, some the size of a man's head; they were at least nine feet tall, with a gate in the middle made from trimmed wooden spars lashed together with rawhide ropes.

Even a cursory glance told Flint that this place must have been here in one form or another for hundreds of years. The Pueblo Indians had been tremendous builders and had created many settlements in the centuries before the white man had settled the West; this was probably an example of their work.

With a ready-built fortification like this already in existence the North would have been mad not to annex it during the Civil War, but he could see why it would have been abandoned once the war was ended, as being too much of an outpost.

Then he saw a sight that chilled him to the bone. There was a metal cage hanging down from the side of the building a few yards from the gate. The cage was swinging back and forth a little in the breeze, the bars streaked with rust, showing that it had been there for quite a while. Interesting though the outside of the artefact was, Flint was more taken by the remains inside the cage. It held the skeleton of a man. There was not enough room for it to fall down, so it was still standing. But this wasn't one of the clean specimens of skeleton you might have seen in the desert. This one still wore extremely tattered remnants of a dark shirt and brown corduroy trousers. White bones gleamed through the tattered fabric and wisps of hair still clung to the bony skull. One arm stuck through the bars in mute supplication, as if they could still do something for him at this late stage in his career. The intention of this display was obvious enough. They were looking at a warning sign.

Well, at least now that they were here, their blindfolds removed, they would have the shackles taken off too, thought Flint with some degree of relief. The metal was digging into his flesh even through the material of his trousers; worn for too long it would have been crippling.

Wrong again. He felt a violent shove in his back and staggered forward as far as the chain that connected his legs would allow.

'Come on, son, we ain't got all day.'

The three of them hobbled through the gates. To their left was a large building that had obviously once contained the administration area of the fort. Outside was a flagpole where once the Union flag would have fluttered proudly. The flagpole was bare. They made slow progress now, having no choice left other than to go forwards. Flint was not too worried about the skeleton they had seen once he got over the initial shock of its being there, but he worried about the effect that it would have on Matt, who might have the body of a grown man but, inside his head, was still a child.

The building had three wide steps. They managed to get up these by being careful with the chain that connected the shackles. If the right leg was lifted too far as you stepped up it would take the left one out from under you. Then they were in the building. Brogan ushered them into a large room with a dimly lit interior and spoke directly to a shadowy figure behind a large oak desk.

'Chief, I've got them here, the ones who killed our men just over a month ago.'

CHAPTER FIVE

The broad windows of the room had long red drapes across them, curtains left over from the days when this had been Fort Lincoln. They had been drawn so they cut out about seventy per cent of the sunlight, and the desk had been angled so that it was away from the direct light.

'So these are the ones?' The figure behind the desk got up and stood in front of them. Only meagre sunlight came through, and their eyes had not yet adjusted to the poor light, so that that his face was still hidden from them. But he was tall and slim with the kind of snake hips you often saw in the more aristocratic kind of Mexican. His voice was soft, with only a lingering accent on the 's' to show that he was indeed a native Spanish speaker. Flint had not been afraid of Brogan when they first met because he had known that type of bully before, but on hearing this softly spoken man he felt a chill go up his back.

'Pull the drapes a little,' said Ramirez. 'Let us see what we are getting.' A figure in the shadows at the back of the room obeyed and the sunlight came streaming through. It was late afternoon so it was not as bright as it would have been earlier in the day, or as hot.

Ramirez was over six feet tall. He wore an ivory-coloured shirt fastened at the wrists with cuff links. His trousers were dark and his feet were clad in boots of finely cured Spanish leather. His black wavy hair was brushed away from his face, and was greying at the sides. Flint would have put him any-where between his late thirties and early forties. His face was long and clean-shaven. Flint could imagine that this service was carried out for him by one of his trusted men using a cut-throat razor and lather created from a well-made soap bought in town and applied with a shaving brush lined with hog bristles.

There was a silvery sheen to the skin of the man that drew Flint's attention. This sheen was apparent both on his hands and his face and even what Flint could see of his neck and chest, for the man wore his shirt partially open, as if to let his fragile skin breathe. With the sharp vision of youth, Flint could see that the man had minute breaks in his skin, one or two of which seemed to be weeping fine pus. He also noted how Ramirez carefully kept out of direct sunlight, sitting once more behind his desk. It was obvious that the bandit leader had a skin condition that reacted badly to the sun. He was whiter than many of the people who were ordi-nary settlers. Flint did not know why he found the discovery of the skin condition unsettling, but he did.

The worst part of this strange figure was his eyes. The eyelids had a slight bulge about them and were half-closed all the time. This gave him an even more reptilian look, especially when it could be seen that his black eyes had hardly any whites to them. This intensified his gaze, as if he was staring straight into the core of these new intruders.

'So, what have you to say about my men?' As he asked the

question Ramirez picked up an object from the polished surface of his desk, a knife. For a moment it caught what little light was still reflected to his desk, and Flint was able to see that the handle was a moulded, grinning skull.

'I don't know what you're talking about.'

This was Flint's automatic gambit. He was sure that by being in denial they would be told much more about what the leader actually knew. Instead Ramirez shrugged his slight shoulders.

'That is fine; you can be taken off and flayed now.' He seemed entirely unaffected by the fact that he had just condemned three men to a brutal and inhumane torture.

'Wait, I might have something to tell you,' said Flint. For his own part he might have bluffed out the situation a little bit longer, but as far as he was concerned he was now responsible for Ty and Matt. 'Who told you about us?'

'That is not your concern at the moment,' said the leader. 'Just tell me the truth, my young friend.'

Flint had a sudden and overwhelming insight into what was happening. Ramirez did not have a clue what had happened to his men. He might have heard rumours through other men who had been to town, but really he was testing them, pure and simple. Flint decided that it was time for him to tell an edited version of the truth.

'Was one of your men tall, a cowboy type, balding at the front?'

'Lucas,' snarled Brogan.

'Too big for his pants, was he?'

'You could say that.'

'Well, we encountered him all right, didn't we, boys?' As he said this Flint looked to either side, the mute appeal asking them to back him up.

'Sure,' said Ty firmly.

'I guess,' mumbled Matt.

'Sure we met him – and his companions. Guess you boys up here must be running out of resources.'

'Why do you say that?' asked Ramirez.

'Well, they was in one of the ranches down on the plain and it sure looked like they wanted some female companionship. They was about to take what they wanted when the three of us came in. Matter could of been settled peaceable-like, but they didn't feel that was too much of a good idea.'

'So they attacked you?' asked Brogan.

'Well, that big fellow you called Lucas seemed to have it in his head that we was wanting some of the spoils. Such a thing never entered our minds, but he decided to give us an early grave. We did what we could in the circumstances.'

The look on Brogan's broad face was a picture. Fury swam across his countenance.

'I told them bastards to never mind the locals, just like you asked us to do.'

'What happened then?'

'Well, the ranch owner was so grateful he gave us a job. Though we don't mind working we're after bigger things, so we thought we'd sound you out. So here we are.' While he was talking Flint had been looking beyond the bandit leader and was startled to see a beautiful face come swimming out of the darkness at the back of the room. The contrast between the light coming in and the figure standing shaded to one side of the drapes meant he had not seen her before.

Ramirez was a man who was acutely aware of what was going on around his sphere of influence; it was what had helped him to survive for so long.

'Come forward, my dear,' he said. The woman who emerged from the darkness at the back of the room was stunning to look at. She was a raven-haired beauty, with very red lips that had been enhanced somehow; she had large dark eyes, and a figure to write home about. The first word that came to Flint's mind was 'curvy' and he saw no reason to alter this at any later time. It was like finding a rose in the middle of the desert, seeing such an exotic creature in such inauspicious surroundings. She wore a dark, flowing dress, and seemed perfectly at ease with the looks of astonishment on their faces. But for all that she was only about the same age as Flint.

'My name is Justine,' she said in a soft voice. Flint pricked up his ears at the tone: she was a Southerner too, not Mexican as might have been thought from a first glance. He took his hat off to her, and so did his companions, a courtesy they had not extended to her leader.

'I think we've already been introduced to you, ma'am,' he said. She gave him a glance of light amusement.

'I think you could say so.'

'That will do for now,' said Ramirez, and the girl retreated away from them, staying in the background, watching what the men were doing. Her presence was another goad to those present, as if they had to prove something in front of her. Flint had a sudden sense of relief. Would the bandit leader introduce them to his companion when he was about to have them killed?

'What do you think, Brogan?' It was obvious that Ramirez had some sort of regard for the big man. Brogan had been standing beside them, but he now took position beside the desk and eyed up the three of them.

'You swear it's the truth? They started it?'

'Dead Mexicans and a girl who was being violated, does that answer your question?' said Flint.

'Yep, that's how it came about,' agreed Ty. Matt just

nodded wordlessly. Brogan came forward without another word – he was not a man to state the obvious – and released them one at a time from their shackles, rattling the chained restraints into the corner for later collection.

'OK, we'll take your word for it,' said Brogan, looking at the man beside him for guidance.

'Before we can accept you we need to see what special – ah – qualities you can bring to our leetle organization.' It was only on one word that Ramirez betrayed his origins. He pointed the knife at Ty Landis. 'You, what are your abilities?' Understandably Ty looked slightly astonished at being questioned in this way.

'Roping,' he said. 'Bit of a gunman.' Like many of his type he was naturally taciturn and did not like to boast of the abilities that had kept him alive for so long.

'Then show us.'

Brogan went off and found a rope. Such things were not hard to come by since the rope was one of the most useful tools at the disposal of any cowboy or bandit. Ty took the rope and expertly made it into a lariat with a slip knot. It was obvious that he was not thinking much about what he was doing; just letting his natural ability take over. The place contained other chairs too, obviously a legacy from the days when the officers would meet here to decide strategy or, more likely, just to smoke big cigars and banter while their men sweated under the hot sun. Ty gave an expert flick of the wrist and his lariat settled across the upright part of the chair. He gave another flick and it spun across the room to land at his feet. The clattering noise this made on the scuffed floorboards was like thunder rolling across the sky.

'That's enough, I can see just from the way you do it that you can rope anything,' said the leader. 'Now, Brogan, give him his gun back.'

Brogan looked a little angry at this, but did as he was asked, first taking out the bullets.. He handed the butt of the weapon to Landis, who holstered it without even looking.

'Draw on each other at my count,' ordered Ramirez.

They did as they were asked to do, the big lieutenant and the slim gunfighter. The gun seemed to jump into Landis's hand with hardly any movement on his part. Three times more they did this and Landis beat the other man every time.

As an onlooker Flint realized that they had not been in as much danger as they thought on the mountain, because Landis would have plugged either of the bandits in their respective foreheads long before they were able to shoot down his small party.

Brogan did not look too happy, and it was obvious that he wanted to continue, but he stood down after a stern look from their leader. Flint did not like the way Brogan regarded Ty at that point, because it was obvious that the second in command did not like being beaten at his own game. Ramirez focused his gaze on Harper.

'What kind of skills can you bring to me?'

Matt was looking as if he was not going to give too good an account of what he could do. Then he received help from an unexpected source.

'When he was getting manacled he punched one of my men about ten feet along from where he was standing. I'd say this one is a pretty impressive close-up fighter.'

Ramirez, who was playing almost hypnotically with the silver-bladed dagger, looked interested at this.

'Many seem to think that guns are the best weapon ever invented, but you can dodge bullets, and ammunition runs out. The fists are a weapon that will last as long as the person does not succumb to gunfire. This is a valuable skill. You will do well, my young friend.' Matt gave a grunt and a nod, but the redness had left his features and it was obvious he was more at ease.

'Now, what skills can you bring to me?' Ramirez looked directly at Flint, who was standing squarely in front of the desk.

'Gunplay, knife skills and planning,' said Flint smartly, knowing that he was really addressing a commanding officer.

'Really? Knives?' said Ramirez. Flint felt a sudden, tiny breeze against the left-hand side of his face and turned. The skull-handled knife was embedded in the oak-panelled door of the office. He put up his hand and pulled the knife away; his hand was red with blood from where the knife had nicked the very tip of his ear.

'If I had taken the lobe away your shoulder would be drenched in blood.' commented Ramirez.

Flint stood very still at this point. If any other man had dared to do such a thing to him that man would now be lying dead with a knife embedded in his heart. But if he killed this leader he would be killed in turn by Brogan. Even if they escaped they had nowhere to go. Worst of all, he would lose his chance to get the gold he so eagerly sought.

'I can sense your hatred of what I have just done,' said Ramirez. 'I have no problem with anger and hatred. They are good if they are channelled to their proper ends. Now gentlemen, I will state plainly what is going on here. This is a revolutionary army and you have been recruited in consequence of your actions today. You will receive fair pay for what you do – certainly better than the stipend given out by the regular army – and I ask in return for your loyalty. Because you are now soldiers army rules will apply to you.

You must obey orders as you would in any army. If you steal or desert the punishment is a court martial and then a flogging if found guilty. If you are treacherous you will be killed by hanging or firing squad.' He gave a faint smile that once more sent a shiver up Flint's back.

'But I will not do you an injustice on your first day. Brogan will take you away and show you your quarters and introduce you to the other men.'

As he spoke the young woman walked with a lazy sway over to the door and detached the knife before taking it back to her leader. Flint managed to keep his eyes forward, even though just looking at her was a temptation. She brushed lightly against him as he passed and he detected a floral perfume that made his senses dance.

'I don't understand,' said Flint, just as it looked as though the second in command was going to lead them away.

'What do you not understand?' asked Ramirez, his grin tightening a little. Brogan shot the young cowboy a warning glance but Flint was genuinely puzzled.

'What is it all for?' he asked, annoyed by the fact that the word 'gold' had not been mentioned once. 'I mean, it seems like a lot of bother to go to just to carry out a few robberies. What do we get out of it?'

'You will be amply rewarded for what you do,' said Ramirez. Brogan suddenly had a frozen look on his features as of one who was detecting the start of a well-worn rant.

'So, my friend, what is eet for?' Ramirez was now building up steam as he rose from behind the dark wood of the desk. As his anger rose the odd word slipped from standard English and his origins became all too recognizable. 'What this is for, is the rescue of this territory from what it has become. You only care about money, but I will make you care for something much higher – a cause. For so many years this area has been mismanaged. Well, I – with the aid of my loyal lieutenants – will foment a revolution that will make this country what it should be.'

'What should it be, then?'

'A place that is governed by the strong, not the weak, a place where men can live in security and know that their government will be behind them in every way. That is why in these very mountains I have stockpiled a treasure – gold, surely, but much more too in the way of weapons and currency. The time has to be right, and that time is now fast approaching.'

The girl, Justine, came forward and laid a slim hand on the jefe's arm; a gold ring set with a red agate stone sparkled on her second finger.

'Juán, calm down; you know what this does to you, along with the heat.'

Ramirez sat down breathing heavily, his thin body trembling, his eyes almost closed. The silver dagger clattered to the surface of the desk. With an effort he sat bolt upright and stared challengingly at the new arrivals.

'You have arrived at an auspicious time, my friends; you are going to see me elected the first president of a new country within weeks, not years!'

Once more, as they were led out of the room, Flint felt a chill sweep down his spine as they left behind a moneyed madman. He wondered, not for the first time, what they had let themselves in for.

CHAPTER SIX

They were soon introduced to the rest of the men who manned the fort. It seemed that they were as mixed a bunch as you would meet anywhere in the four territories. Some of them were former Mexican vaqueros, but surprisingly most came from the Southern states, making up a band of about thirty men in all. Some of the men were silent and hostile, others seemed friendlier, but with a glint in their eyes that indicated that they would not suffer fools gladly. The newcomers were looked upon with suspicion while Brogan took them for a tour of the fort.

The building they had been in was indeed the command centre and the officers' quarters for the camp. It was not an especially big construction, made as it was from a mixture of adobe, brick, and wood. The roof was flat with drainage pipes at intervals to take away the excess water from the monsoon rain.

Not far from the main building was a partially covered pit about eight feet deep dug into the rocky ground. This was big enough to take about ten men. At first Flint could not see the reason for its being there, but the man showing them around saw his puzzled expression.

'That's for special punishment, teach the bad 'uns a lesson,' he said. 'Any man spends a couple of nights in there he'll do what he's told.' Flint could imagine being there in the pitiless heat of the day, and felt a slight shudder between his shoulder blades at the thought.

A corral had been created further on, across from the main building; this contained many kinds of horses including quarter horses, sorrels and greys, but the greatest number among them were mustangs, the hardy little horses that were usually found on the plains but could adapt to any other kind of territory.

Also near the main building was the cookhouse and bakery; the centre of operations in a place like this. This was manned by Chinese cooks who seemed quite pleased to ply their trade despite the fact they were working for criminals. This was no reflection on them: one boss was probably much the same as another.

Across from the cookhouse by about the span of a main street was an arsenal. It was easy to tell how precious this was to the bosses because it was guarded, both day night, by two men carrying carbines.

Further on were two bunkhouses set at an angle to each other. These were also made of adobe and obviously housed the majority of the men. There was another building standing in the shelter of one of the walls, about the same length as one of the bunkhouses, but with two floors instead of one. This housed some whom Flint rapidly thought of as 'camp followers,' because he was uneasy about labelling them as what they were in his mind: a bunch of whores brought here by promise of easy money and often kept here by their inability to get away.

'This is where you eat,' said Brogan, bringing them into a kind of mess hall which would have been used by the soldiers. The furnishings were not fancy: plain wooden benches set at equally rough long tables that were scarred by years of men chipping at the wood while yarning over their meals, and the depredations of the inevitable beetles.

'You can even get a beer,' said Brogan, pointing to the

barrels in the corner. 'But not too much, and no spirits, Ramirez don't approve of 'em. Whiskey steals your brain an' puts a fightin' devil in there. Now I'll show you your quarters.'

'I've slept in many a bunkhouse,' said Ty, in a slightly lofty manner. He couldn't help his ways, thought Flint, since his betrayal by his wife he had been pretty much detached from the human race. This just seemed like another thing for him to do.

'That's as maybe,' said Brogan, leading them out into the sunshine, 'but you're not in there, you're out in the encampment at the back.' He led them to a bunch of sorry-looking canvas tents out at the back of the bunkhouses and pretty well up against the far wall of the fort. 'These are empty for the present, so grab one each if you want. Oh, and I wouldn't go wandering around too much during the night; we post guards every hour of the clock. Anyway, you boys can set a campfire and gab later, we're going back to get you some work.'

There was always something to be done in a settlement the size of this one that must have numbered over sixty people in total including those who weren't actually in the bandit business. Getting enough food for the horses was a major headache, solved by taking them out and leading them to grass on the slopes, as well as gathering said grass in bales and ripening it for feed. Feeding the inhabitants of the fort also presented a problem. At least once a week they had to go and fetch supplies from one of the three towns, paying in cash and leading their packhorses up the trail. In addition men went out every day with rifles and shot anything they could find up to and including bears. In actual fact a nice juicy bear steak was looked on with favour in the encampment and was said to be one of Ramirez's favourite meals.

The only animals that were not shot were rabbits and birds, since the average bullet would blow them apart and render the carcass unfit for consumption. These animals were trapped with wires and snares.

Brogan got together his two men – the new recruits were still unarmed – and took them out to a rather unusual plateau about half a mile away and forty feet high, that sat even above the fort. An easy climb led up the side of this small mesa.

'Master's Point,' he grunted as he showed them to the top. 'We have a lookout here during the daylight hours.' The Point was made of red stone, at the top it was shaped rather like a shallow boat and not much wider. But it was at least thirty feet long and commanded a field of vision that no one else could get unless they were here, allowing a panoramic view of their surroundings. The guard who was present gave Brogan a brief salute and looked suspiciously at the visitors. From his waist hung, of all things, a slightly tarnished trumpet.

'If we are attacked we will not be taken unawares,' said the big man in a cheerful manner that hinted at his doubt that it would happen at all. Flint reserved judgement. He had other thoughts on his mind.

He noticed that the Point overlooked another mesa a quarter of a mile away. He could also see that in the side of the mesa was one of the buildings constructed so long ago by the stone-age people who had lived here. It was not a remarkably impressive structure, just a building of lighter grey stone that went back into the mesa below the rim of the flattened hill, the doorway and the windows blocked off long ago for some obscure reason. This area was filled with such artefacts so he paid little attention to this one.

'Make yourself familiar with the place,' said Brogan, 'but

don't get too comfortable. There'll be real work for you to do – and soon.' He left them soon afterwards, apparently satisfied with his new recruits. Clearly discipline was not that tight, unlike in the real army, until a person was called upon to do his duty.

When the three of them got back to their accommodation Flint had to marvel at the amount of space inside his tent. You could have housed a small family in there, which, he supposed, might have been the original idea. He left the other two and took a walk around the fort, making himself familiar with the layout of the place. He quickly discovered that the walls were not in as good order as he had imagined. A lot of debris from carcasses and other food sources had been dumped against the main wall near the kitchen, which made that area stink to high heaven. Old wheels, bits of rusty metal and clothes also lay about near the bunkhouses. The place was a rubbish dump.

In addition the walls were not as well protected as might have been expected. At intervals the wall had been breached both by time and weather. The rains were mainly to blame for the crumbling fabric. Flint could well imagine that over the course of many years even the toughest wall could give way to erosion, especially when aided by the corrosive effects of the sun and the invasive plants that worked their roots under the structure. Near the back of the encampment he found one such breach as wide as a large door but with uneven edges, which led straight out to the hills, and he understood at once why Ramirez wasn't too worried. Such a breach would be accessible to only one or two men at a time and could be easily covered by someone with a rifle, instead of having to go to all the trouble of shoring up the gap. But it gave him an idea. On the morrow he would see if he could liberate his horse and have him handy for any adventures they might need to go on.

When night came, in common with his friends he took sole possession of his tent. The interior of the tent was dark as he lay wrapped in a large woven blanket. He almost felt rather than saw the figure that stole through the dimly lit entrance. Flint was asleep, but he woke and was ready for action at the same time. Detecting the intruder by breath alone, he pounced, knife in hand ready to slit the throat of anyone who would have slain him. This was not a feeling that was to last long as he found himself with an armful of warm, curvy woman. She had given a quick shriek of dismay, but he was already pulling away from her.

'Sorry, I didn't know it was you.' He lit an oil lamp that had a low flame and set it between them. She was not looking frightened now; in fact he could tell even in the dim light that she was quite excited to be here.

'What the hell do you want?' he asked in his ordinary voice. She quickly put a hand over his mouth.

'Shhh, talk as low as you can, cowboy.' Her own tone was hushed, almost reverential.

'But what do you want?'

'This.' She leaned in and kissed him on the lips. The touch of her mouth against his was almost too much for his senses. Even her breath was sweet and sweet breath was something you wouldn't get very much around here. His senses were aroused in more ways than one and he pushed her away from him, not roughly but reluctantly.

'Are you trying to get us killed, ma'am?'

'Not if you keep quiet and just get on with it.'

'Listen, I might be slow in the head over some things, but you just don't walk into some place and steal el gran jefe's woman. That way, when he finds out you're mighty liable to find your carcass riddled with lead, and I want to keep this hide intact.'

'All right, cowboy, I won't press you. I like you, Texas, I can tell by your accent you come from the hill country; well, so do I. You think you can just walk in here and settle down?'

'I suppose we just did.'

'You think so? The minute Brogan met you and your men he had plans for the three of you. He never intended to kill you, he just did that to put the fear of your lives in you and make you obedient.'

'Guess I figured that much out on my own.'

'Ramirez needs men all the time. He even sends out a few on a recruitment drive in the bigger towns.'

'Well, why would that be?'

'Because a lot of 'em get shot dead or hung when they're caught.'

Flint had figured out that much, too. Being a bandit was not a safe career choice. Too many things could go wrong even when you planned everything down to the last detail. It just took a store clerk with a rifle behind the counter or a bank worker with a concealed handgun to bring your career to an abrupt end. Not to mention the law.

'Not a real surprise there,' said Flint.' Now, you leave and hope that no one saw you coming in here, for both our sakes.'

'Let me help you before I go. Brogan needs new men, but he also needs to put them to the test. Tomorrow he's going to do precisely that.'

'And what form does this test take?'

'He's going to ask you to ride a few miles north of here to the settlement of Hope Springs.'

'What kind of place is that?'

'It's a mining community. They're looking for gold in the

57

hills. As you know this area's rich in minerals. The trouble is they might find something.'

'Why would that be a problem?'

'Well, the minute land becomes valuable all sorts of things happen. The government, who left them to their own devices, will suddenly find they have an interest in developments and they'll send in a few officials.'

'Yep, I suppose so.'

'Then, when word gets out there's a claim all sorts will come out of the woodwork. Before you know it Hope Springs will be a proper little town with supply chains, saloons and explorers poking all over the place as the gold or silver – more likely to be silver around these parts – runs out in the first mine.'

She did not have to explain any further. One of the expeditions was bound to come across the fort and find out it was manned. Questions would be asked by the governors and it would be discovered that the criminals had been there for some time. A bunch of bandits could not hold out for long against proper troops, there just weren't enough of them to man the defences. Then there would be an end to the fort, possibly after a siege, so much better to scare off the initial settlers in the first place.

'Brogan's going to tell you that they are rebels who broke away and that we have to take them down by every means. The trouble is, that camp is also full of women and children too; whole families who have decided to explore and make a better life. Brogan doesn't care and neither does Ramirez; they just want to get a lot of trouble off their own doorstep. I don't care what you men do to each other, but I don't like to see innocent people being destroyed.'

'So you came in here just to use me?' asked Flint, a harsh edge to his voice.

'If you think that, you're wrong!' Her temper flared and she glared at him. 'I just want to make sure a lot of innocent people don't die, and if I can have fun persuading you, well, that's a good result.'

'So you really do have a fancy for me?'

'If you're up for it, cowboy.'

'But I still don't see why you should care for a lot of people you've never met. Also I don't see why I should get riddled with lead for making love to the woman of a mad leader. You've just given me the most enjoyable suicide proposition I've ever had.'

'Ramirez is not my lover! He gives everyone that impression because a man as powerful as he is must have a woman like me. The truth is that he cannot function as a man due to his condition, the same condition that makes his skin blister and peel when he is out in the sun. He is a shell of a man and does not satisfy me.'

'If what you say is true then he is even more dangerous than I thought, for he will focus only on power and have no other distractions.'

'As for the settlement, I have an older sister, and she is there with her family. They have young children and I would not see them harmed.'

He now had a reason for believing her. Family ties can be strong to the point where members will die for each other.

'Then they have to be warned.'

She looked at him with those shining eyes as she knelt there on the old horse blanket and he knew what he was going to do even though it might mean the end of all his dreams if he was caught.

'All right, but I'll need a horse.'

'Don't worry, I've already solved that problem; yours is out the back.'

'How do you know he's mine?'

'I had a good look at you boys when you were coming in through the gates. I was brought up with horses, I would know yours from a thousand others, I told the guards I was going for an amble around the outside walls. They just took me at my word.'

'Talking about guards, I've been told someone patrols every hour, and once I'm outside, what if I'm spotted from someone up on the Point?'

'Brogan was just trying to keep you in your place. The guard patrols about once every four hours, and it's one man. As for the Point, there's no one up there,' she said. 'That's only manned during the daylight hours, gets too cold at night. Talking about that, what kind of clothes do you have?'

'I've got woollen chaps,' he said, 'a face protector and gloves. I'll be all right. The encampment's off to the north, you say? What if I get lost?'

'Funnily enough, I don't think you will.'

He got ready, then they went out the back. Sure enough his horse was already there. Some grass grew in the shade of the walls and the horse was cropping this, then he raised his head and gave a snicker in greeting. Flint slapped his neck.

'Good old boy,' he said. Flame was golden-coloured, with a light mane and a defiant yellow blaze on his forehead that had given him his name. Instead of mounting his steed Flint led him towards the crumbling wall, Justine looked at the newcomer with genuine admiration.

'I was just going to show you that; you've obviously worked out a few things for yourself.'

'Yep.' He turned to her as the horse clip-clopped across the sandy soil. 'You best get out of here. If I get caught things'll look bad for you.'

'Thanks,' she said. He felt warm lips against his for a mere second, and then she was gone.

Luckily it was one of those still desert nights when the moon is high in the sky. He led Flame through the gap and out the other side, walking with him for a good five minutes before setting off through the hills to the north. Justine hadn't told him how many miles away the settlement was but it must be close enough for Ramirez to feel threatened. He rode steadily, wondering how he was going to tell a mining community in the middle of the night that they were going to be raided by bandits.

CHAPTER SEVEN

There is always an element of shooting the messenger when bad news has to be imparted to a group of people who would rather not be disturbed in their normal pursuits. It was about one in the morning when Flint rode into the mining camp of Hope Springs. Naturally they had a watchman posted; this was wild country and they were even more nervous than Ramirez because they were exposed to the wilds without any protection.

The camp consisted mostly of tents, hastily built shacks with roofs made of tin or wood, and one or two properly constructed adobe brick buildings. It was early days yet, but there was a feeling that here was a community that might thrive if they did indeed find large mineral deposits.

Flint had tied a bandanna around the lower part of his face. Along with his hat his identity was well concealed. He moved his horse to the lower part of the slope where the guard was standing and ran forward, weapons in hand. The guard had been half-dozing and was startled to find a stranger right in front of him, a gun in each hand. Flint had armed himself because he wanted to immediately control the situation.

'What the hell?' The guard was not without courage, he raised his rifle to point it at the shadowy figure.

'Throw it down,' said Flint. 'or you're a dead man.' It looked for a moment as if the man was going to defy the intruder, then he lowered his weapon.

'We ain't got much,' he said gruffly. 'You're wasting your time.'

'Listen to me,' said Flint. 'Armed robbers, raiders really, are going to come here this very day and burn out your camp. They're going to kill every man, woman and child they come across. Get your women and children away. Stay and fight if you want, but get the ones who can be hurt easy out of here. I mean this.'

'Why should I believe you?'

'Have you ever heard of Ramirez?'

The man became even more watchful.

'Sure, who hasn't? He's a big name in these parts, all sortsa stories.'

'Well, that's who you're up against.'

'Who the blame are you, in the middle of the night, that I should believe you?'

Flint realized that he was being tricked, that the man's voice was getting louder and louder. Already Flint, with his young, superior hearing could hear stirrings from the tents and huts around them. He fired a bullet near the man's foot; the man cursed and jumped away from his rifle. Flint turned and fled down the hill to where his horse had become alert at the sound of gunfire.

With one leap he was on the back of his steed, gathering up the reins as the darkness of the hill came alive with muffled shouts and calls. He knew he had no more than seconds to go before he was caught, so he urged his horse to go forward as fast as he could on what trail there was.

He came to a rise between two hills and only then was he able to spur his steed into a gallop, the going lit by the moonlight that had cast too many shadows lower down. Some of the braver souls from the mining town had managed to saddle up and ride after him – perhaps they were even on bareback? It didn't matter, the result was the same, he was being pursued and their horses were a lot fresher than his. The only plus he had on his side was that, having carried him to this place, Flame seemed to know his way back to the fort as if he had been taking in every little sign on the way here. Flint, once more, was content to give his horse a head start because he knew that Flame was a lot more sensitive than his supposed master was about these things.

Flint was right in one respect though: his pursuers did not want to be drawn too far from their camp for several reasons. They didn't know if this was some sort of trick and someone else was out there to get them. They also didn't know if they would be able to get back from wherever they were being led to in the dark. Flint heard shouts and muffled curses along with a few random shots as his pursuers veered away.

Down in the camp a number of people had gathered in the

light of the oil lamp used by the guard. Their leader was a big man called Edwardes, who was doing his best to deal with the uproar around him.

'Look, ain't no use carrying on like this. We got to organize and sort ourselves out.'

The five men who had been chasing the intruder came back and dismounted in the light of the moon.

'Did you get him?' asked Edwardes.

'Don't reckon we did,' said one of the younger riders. 'We left him when his horse was a distance away. Let a few shots off in his direction, so there's a chance he could be lying out there right now, but I doubt it.'

'So tell me again,' asked Edwardes of the original guard, 'what was that name he gave?'

'Something about a Ramirez who was going to raid the camp,' said the guard. 'Sounded like a bunch of bullcrap to me. Told us to get the women and children away because he's goin' to kill everyone he can get his paws on.'

'Then we take him serious,' said Edwardes. 'Soon as it gets light we gather up all we can get hold of and take the women and children out of here.'

Most of the men were by now gathered around the hill on which the big man stood.

'You know how much bother that's goin' to be? They'll be cold, hungry, have to shelter on the lower slopes,' protested one man. 'Then no raid? All them bothers for nothin'?' There was an angry murmur of agreement.

'All right.' Edwardes held up his hands. 'But what if it's true? What if these heathen bandits ride in and fire up this settlement?'

'We stay and fight!' shouted one man.

'Yep, and with our women and kids here we'll have a lot more to defend, and what if they win? Wouldn't you rather see every last tent and shack gone than risk the lives of our women and children? I say we get them to go! We hide them, and if it doesn't happen we just look foolish. If it does, then there'll be a lot of precious survivors.'

There was a bit more arguing after that over the details of what they were going to take and how they were going to defend their community, but the truth of the matter had struck home. Many of the men had left jobs or smallholdings back South to try and make a better life for themselves and their families. They were willing to tackle mining even though that might be risky, because there might be a big reward at the end. At least that way they were not risking the lives of their families. They were quite well organized because this had been designed as a mining community from the start. Edwardes had quickly seen how men working together could achieve that which they could not do with separate claims. They could pool resources for one thing.

As daylight came the children were dressed in as many clothes as they could get. Tents were rolled up and wives – some protesting vigorously – were led off to a safe place on the wooded lower slopes, where they could hide from a thousand bandits if need be, while those men who were left got ready to defend what was theirs.

One young girl said nothing to her husband, even though she could have protested with the rest as she was led away to the new shelters, especially as she was pregnant. But it was her sister who lived in Rockfort along with the killers.

It was going to be a long wait.

In the meantime Flint had given his horse free rein, which meant that they were back at the fort within an hour. He got the horse to walk sedately to the crumbling region of wall and led him through. Then he did something that would have surprised an observer, should there have been one: he stroked his horse's mane and whispered in his ear. The steed responded with a low whickering noise that sounded like agreement, and then began to make his own way back to the corral.

Flint was far from stupid; even though Justine was gone; he knew that it was she who had liberated his horse. He also knew that if Flame was spotted outside the corral and questions were asked they would quickly come to the conclusion that Justine had become bored with her late-night perambulations and had simply gone to bed, leaving the horse to return on its own, as most horses would.

Flint stole into his tent and lay on the ground still clothed, throwing the blankets around his numb body. It was cold out there in the hills at this time of night and he could hardly feel any of his extremities. His teeth chattered for a long time before there was enough warmth in his body to calm them down. He was tired, but the thought of what he had done came back to him all the time. He had been tricked into doing a good deed when all he was here for was gold. Did he feel good about what he had done? Not really: he felt stupid, used and above all, fearful. If his role in warning the mining community was found out he was dead meat, and Ramirez seemed to have no trouble disposing of those who crossed him.

A long time passed before fitful sleep came his way.

Early in the morning Ty was just turning over for the third time when he felt a hamlike hand shake him awake. He sat bolt upright and jammed the gun he always kept within reach into the short ribs of the person who had roused him.

'It's all right.' Matt pulled away and held up his hands.

'Look, just me. Came to talk to you.'

'What about? An' this better be good. I have things to do, some of 'em fairly urgent.' Ty got up and stretched. He was forty now and his age was beginning to catch up on him.

'I thought I was dreaming last night, but I'm sure I heard voices.'

'So what was it? Angels?'

'No, I think that Flint was up to something.'

'Well why didn't you go and find out about it if you was so curious?'

'I was half-asleep and I drifted off. Must've been well past midnight. Anyways I woke up a lot later and heard Flint whispering again, then the sound of hoofs, and then he went away to his tent.'

'So what?'

'Dunno.' Matt looked miserably at his big hands. 'This isn't real easy for me to say. I don't have a way with words. Mebbe we should stick our lot in with Ramirez?'

'I guess you need to say more.'

'Well, it's like this. We're outsiders. You think down there in the ranch that you're making big plans. Then you get up here and see what it's really like. You get to thinking: maybe this is too big. Do you know what I mean?' Matt lowered his head miserably again.

'Yep, I know exactly what you mean.' Ty lifted his gun and pointed it straight at Matt. 'Explain to me why I shouldn't blow your miserable brains out right now? You want me to betray my friend and lose our one chance for a fortune? I expect I could make it look like an accident.'

'They're too good at what they do. We don't have a chance. One wrong move and they'll blow us off the hills.'

'All right, let's say I think you have a point. I'm not going to betray Flint.'

'I'm not asking you to do that.' Matt paused as he searched for a way to put his case. It took a while because his thought processes were so slow. 'He killed someone who was my friend. This new Brogan is my chance. These people know what they're doing.'

'I think you're making a mistake if you go over to Ramirez,' said Ty evenly. 'He seems to hold all the cards right now with his big plans, but how can I make you see this is just temporary?'

'What do you mean?'

'He's talking revolution, man. When that comes out, if we're on his side we'll be done for.'

'I don't see it.'

'Don't you? Then let me put it plain for you. If the government gets wind of this they'll send troops here as fast as they can. You going to fight a bunch of soldiers with your bare fists?'

'No, I guess not,' mumbled Matt.

'OK then; we do what we have to do and stay as we are, obeying orders like we're supposed to until the time comes when we can do what we want.'

'I guess so,' mumbled Matt. 'Except. . . .'

'What?'

'He killed my friend. I guess he thinks we made up, but he could have knocked him over. He didn't need to do that.'

Ty gave an inward sigh. It looked as if he was never really going to get through to this man. He would have to keep an eye on Matt in case he inadvertently betrayed them all.

'Matt, listen to me, this is very important. If Brogan finds out what happened to his brother he'll blame us all. We'll all be executed. These are people who don't want any doubt hanging around. They won't mark you up as some great hero, believe me, I've seen their kind before.'

'All right.' Matt still looked unconvinced.

They heard shouting in the distance, rapidly coming closer. Brogan appeared at the entrance to the tent.

'You boys got twenty minutes to get ready. We're heading out. See you're having a chinwag. Where's your friend?'

'Asleep,' said Matt.

'Well, he won't be in two minutes.' Brogan tramped off and they could hear him shouting again.

Just as they were ordered, they lined up in the early-morning sun: Flint, Matt, Ty and six bandits, with Brogan completing the ensemble. Flint, standing there having eaten little, was unshaved and still looked tired. Brogan handed them each a Colt .44 and a short cutlass within a belted sheath, which they tied around their waists.

'You boys'll be in the lead,' he said. 'But don't get any ideas about escaping, or shooting your way out. These men can shoot the heads off a pigeon at sixty paces, an' they won't hesitate. Today, boys, is when you're going to prove yourselves.'

Their steeds were brought out for them already saddled, hardy mustangs that could get them there and back without too much trouble. For once Flint was glad that they hadn't given him his own horse. He exchanged glances with Matt, who looked at the ground, then at Ty, who gave him a wry smile. Then they rode out of the main gate, pacing their steeds in the gathering heat of the morning.

CHAPTER EIGHT

Flint was tired but the warming sun and the steady ride rein-vigorated him. They seemed to take a lot longer to get to their target, even though they were going in daylight, and he realized there was a reason for this. The horses had not been this way before and, as always, their pace was dictated by the slowest rider, who was Matt, while Flint had been able to give his steed permission just to go as fast as he wanted. Luckily they had water containers made from hide with them and were able to stop and refresh themselves on the way.

In the back of his mind Flint hoped that the settlers had taken his warning seriously, or all the effort made and the tiredness he felt would have been for nothing. Innocent lives would be lost. He took little comfort from the fact that to protect themselves, as they saw it, the bandits would have carried out this raid anyway.

A while later they were at the mining community. Between two of the hills was a mine-working carved into the side of the rocky material. This was where the settlers had discovered the silver that that was going to make their fortune. Brogan halted his men and gave them some last-minute instructions. Then he got Flint to ride beside him and they swept down into the village. The rest of the men followed, roaring and whooping to make the maximum amount of noise.

Miners who had been hiding behind the makeshift build-ings began to fire on the intruders, but the bandits were going too fast to be hit effectively, especially when those firing at them were inexperienced at using weapons. These were peaceful miners, not cowboys or gunmen.

Strangely enough, Flint found himself getting caught up in the heat of the moment. He threw himself off his horse when he was in the middle of the encampment and winged a man who had jumped up from behind one of the shacks. Flint took out his cutlass and ran around the camp, laying not into the men but their tents. He was an accurate shot and did not kill those who opposed him, but left them unable to fight with a shot to the upper arm or the lower leg. Flint also discovered that he was able to knock down the ramshackle buildings with help from the other men who had also dismounted, kicking into the fabric of the huts so that they fell down.

Matt had jumped into a group of four men, punching out as he landed amongst them, quickly laying out all four on the dusty ground.

The miners had been dealt with quickly. Injured, disabled men lay everywhere. Now Brogan went to the campfire in the centre of the village and used the burning brands to set fire to any building that was still standing. They had not seen a single woman or child, and in his heart Flint felt a swelling pride that he had at least saved a few innocent lives.

Then there came the crack of a rifle from one of the surrounding hills. Someone cannier than his fellows had taken up a concealed position amongst the rocks. One of the bandits give a scream of pain as his chest erupted with a great spurt of his lifeblood and he fell face down in the soil.

Brogan was the biggest of the men and he was standing beside the one who had just been killed. The big man looked over at the hills and began to take out his weapon which he had so recently reholstered while looking over his work in the camp. There was another crack from the concealed gunman in the hills and Brogan suddenly felt his feet being taken out from under him. He landed with a huge thud on his back, staring up at the darkly clad man who had tackled him to the ground. While they were still in motion they both heard the sharp crack of the rifle again and the bullet passed harmlessly overhead where, just a minute before, it would have hit Brogan in the chest. Another figure ran in between the prone men and the gunman, Ty Landis raised his gun and fired. There was a wild yell of pain from the hills and the lone gunman was no more. Brogan got to his feet, dusted down his big body and gave Flint a nod of thanks, no more, then ordered his men to mount their horses, since all the unwounded miners had fled.

They also took away the body of the dead bandit. They left the living but wounded men alone. As far as the attackers were concerned they needed survivors to spread the word about what had happened to this would-be community. Men would risk a lot if they thought they might be able to get some kind of wealth; what they would not risk was the certainty of being attacked and killed by those who wanted to keep these hills. This was not some Indian tribe who had attacked them, but people with superior fire power and secure headquarters, people who could come back again and again to an area that had never been properly explored. In his own mind Brogan was satisfied that they had dealt a death blow to this community.

They rode back to the fort under the afternoon sun, stopping now and then for water. It would have been impossible to cross the desert down below at this time of day, but up here in the hills the sun was not as warm, and cool breezes blew between the rolling dips in the landscape.

Ramirez was waiting in his usual place when the men were brought to him. They stood in front of his desk. Flint saw that Justine was in the background as usual. He had a feeling that she had to be here when the leader was meeting with other people. She gave him a cool look as if she recalled him vaguely from somewhere else and he played to this by giving her one glance, then ignoring her altogether.

'Was the raid successful?' Ramirez asked his lieutenant.

'Yes,' said Brogan, describing the breaking-up of the camp.

'Did these men play a full part?'

'Yep, they were active. This man, Joe Flint, along with Landis here, saved my life. And the way Matt used his fists was a mighty good sight to see.'

'Well, looks as if you have become part of our little band of brothers,' said Ramirez. He had some warmth in his voice, which only meant it was a little less than icy. 'See that you do as you're told. Thank you for saving Brogan, he's very useful to me. I would have missed him for that reason.'

Brogan gave a tight smile at this, which said to them that he knew his boss was only kidding, but he didn't like it just the same.

'OK you boys,' he said. 'You can go and get some food, then we'll see what we can plan for you to do.'

It was strange for the three of them to walk out of the main building without an escort. The other two went for something to eat, but Flint had a drink from the well in the middle of the fort, then went for a walk around the walls to try and get to know the place even better. As he had suspected when he had looked around the other day, the place was really not in a good condition Much of the wall was crumbling at the top. The lack of manpower – the place really was too big for about sixty people – meant that nothing was getting done in the way of repairs.

The rebel fort contained a varied assortment of men who, when they were not out raiding, mostly sat at the doorway of the mess hall smoking, drinking beer and regaling each other with their stories of the past. Pleasant though these activities were, Flint knew that he wanted to catch up with his sleep, so he was going to head for his bed. He noticed that the few women in the camp also acted as servants for the men, bringing them food and beer, so they did not have to move about much. It made sense in a community like this one that these violent individuals were waited on, because they were prone to sudden mood shifts and they were dangerous men.

Three of them sat outside the old mess hall. As Flint looked on a young girl came across from the kitchen and served them some fried steak. The girl was young, trim, and held herself very well. The three men insulted her with suggestions that had more to do with bed than food. She ignored them and walked away, passing within a few feet of Flint.

'Morven!' he said in a low voice. 'What the hell are you doing here?'

The girl looked at him blankly, as if they had never met before.

'I'm sorry; you must have mistaken me for someone else. But if you want to talk I'll meet you near the cathouse.' This was the name of the place where the women lived and consorted with the men. 'I'll see you in about an hour.' She nodded to him and left on her food mission.

Flint did not linger either. He did not want to endanger her in any way by hanging around and calling attention to their arrangement. His mind was in turmoil. Of all the people he might have seen here she was the least expected. She must have come here shortly after they had left Hadfield Drake's ranch.

Instead of going to his bed for a few hours as he had planned he got some food in the mess hall with the rest of the men. Matt was looking pretty pleased at this turn of events. He had been accepted and he was being fed, both reasons for settling down in a place where his unique talents were not just tolerated, but encouraged. He did not seem troubled that they had broken up a settlement of people who might have made a thriving community up here in the hills, but seemed only concerned about where his next beer might come from. Ty was a lot more troubled about the whole business. He was careful not to express his doubts to Flint, but destroying the living of others did not sit well with him.

After exchanging a few pleasantries and finding his body considerably refreshed by the food, Flint strolled over to where the whores granted an open gateway to their charms. The girl, who was standing talking to an older woman when Flint appeared, excused herself and came over to see him.

'Look as though we're drifting towards the building,' she said. He obeyed, following her slowly, both of them talking in low voices as if engaged in some mutually beneficial negotiations.

'What the hell are you doing here?' asked Flint.

'Right off, you talk to me like that I'll just walk away and have nothing to do with you,' said the girl.

'Sorry, I'm just worried about you being here. What happened?'

'Shortly after you left my father became ill. He ...' her eyes filled with tears. 'He took some kind of heart attack. Within hours of you leaving he was dead. There wasn't a thing we could do. It was all the problems, they got to him.'

'That's terrible,' said Flint.

'I'd already told Father I didn't want to be at the ranch any more, that I didn't feel safe. He'd arranged before he fell ill to give me a couple of servants to take me to the nearest town, where I was going to get a stagecoach to Tucson. We were waylaid by bandits who decided they needed more . . . ladies, up here.'

'So you didn't come here on purpose?'

'No – I did come here deliberately. I rode off in a direction I knew the bandits often came from. I misled our servants. I didn't resist when I was brought here to be part of this. I could have fought back; there was a chance we could have got away.'

'But why would you want to be here?'

She looked at him with those big, clear eyes. She really was a very pretty girl and he found he was captivated once more by her. He would forgive a girl like that almost anything, even being as foolhardy as she had shown herself to be.

'I want to kill their leader.'

'What?'

'The more I thought about what those men had done at my father's ranch, the angrier I became. I've got nothing to live for any more. Why should I have been exposed to that because some greedy, lying robber sits in his little nest like a rattlesnake and terrorizes the country? Do you know what you do with a sidewinder? You shoot off its head.'

'But if you do that you'll be killed too.'

'No I won't, because you're going to help me.'

'Wait a minute. How could you make me part of your plan? You didn't even know I was here until we met.'

'Yes I did. I heard you making some of your plans with

the other two back down at the ranch. You want gold; I want to destroy this place that has brought so much misery to other people.'

'You've got to get out of here,' said Flint. 'It's as simple as that. This place isn't as secure as it seems to be. I'll get you out in the next couple of days.'

'You're wrong. I'm staying and completing the job.' Flint realized that the two of them were starting to raise their voices, which was not a good idea in a place like this. A couple of the women lounging in the door of the cathouse were staring at him; he knew that they could summon help if they thought the girl was being threatened.

'Ah, see you've met my new gal,' said a hearty voice. It was Shaun Brogan, looming over the two of them. He came straight up to Morven and wrapped his arm around her waist, pulling her into him. 'She's a beauty, ain't she? Brand new.' It was obvious he was not looking on the new arrival for mere companionship. The girl smiled up at him in a way that made the hairs rise on the back of Flint's neck.

'Let her go,' said Flint, stepping back. It was a badge of his new acceptance that he now carried a gun. His hand hovered over his holster.

'Whoah cowboy!' said Brogan. 'She's fresh meat; don't get het up.'

'She's mine,' said Flint. 'Go ahead, we'll see who wins.'

They stared at each other with narrowed eyes. Brogan pushed the girl to one side and faced Flint square on.

'You want a fight over a woman, son?'

'Not really. I don't think it's worth our while,' said Flint, 'but she's mine all right.' He relaxed and took his hand away from his gun. The girl came to his side. Brogan looked from one youthful face to the other, then suddenly gave a wry laugh.

'I see what it is. Well, I guess the old saw is true, youth to youth. OK, you win for now. I'm no mood for a fight after today, not when you done so well out there.' His eyes narrowed again. 'But there was somethin' wrong with that raid. Things didn't feel right. Would you know anythin' about that?'

'I'll just go and get a few things done,' said the girl. She looked significantly at Flint. 'I'll see you later.' He gave her a brief nod, then she was gone.

'Well, do you know anythin'?'

'What do you mean?' Flint was playing for time.

'When we come to these places they're unprepared usually, maybe there's a couple of lookouts who try and get the rest into action.'

'So?'

'Hope Springs didn't feel like that, did it?'

'Don't know. I relied on you, Brogan, because you have the nous. I'm new here, I can't tell what's right or wrong 'cause I've never done it before.'

'You look mighty young; quiet too,' said Brogan, 'but I have a feeling that we've got to keep an eye on you, that you could be trouble in the future.'

'I'm just here for what the rest of you want, a new start, a girl, and money. There's nothin' to it, really.'

'I'll turn it over in my mind, what happened on that raid. We can't leave things like that to chance. If they start regrouping and come back, we'll have to go out there and do the same again, and I don't want to spare the manpower. Besides, I lost a good man today.'

'When is he getting buried?'

'Buried?' Brogan stared at Flint as if he was joking. 'We took everything useful offa him and threw his naked carcass down a gully. He'll be picked clean in a couple of days.'

'I have an explanation of why they might have been ready for you,' said Flint.

'That's interesting. What?'

'Maybe they had heard rumours about the fort, including the fact that Ramirez is a merciless killer. Maybe they were so keyed up about that fact that they were at the ready for the last few days. It sure looked to me as if they had suspended operations on the mine.'

'So? What does that have to do with anything?'

'Well, maybe their community leaders decided that, since they were not getting much joy over finding minerals, they would rouse them up, distract them with the idea that they were going to be raided by us. Maybe it was on their minds long before it happened.'

'Could be, I suppose. So what do you think that means for Hope Springs?'

'I think it means that they'll fold up their tents and go as far away from that district as possible. Not only that, they'll spread stories about what we did and they'll put other people off coming back to look for gold or silver.' He found it easy enough to sound sincere, because in point of fact this was what he actually believed.

'OK, I'll take your word for it now,' Brogan seemed pleased. Flint was careful not to let the relief show on his tanned features. 'All right,' Brogan went on, 'got to go, but once you finish with that little lady, leave some for me.' He turned, and went striding off. Flint felt almost weak, trembling from the body juices that were telling him to flee from this place for ever.

Maybe he should have listened.

Instead he went to look for the girl.

CHAPTER NINE

More than a week passed in the fort. During that time Matt, Ty and Flint became as much part of the company as anybody who had been there. Flint found out that Morven was not really as willingly his girl as she might have seemed. In fact they did not have a physical relationship at all, even though he was seen as her protector. In some ways this suited him, because he was frustrated and annoyed with her over her stubborn refusal to give up her plans to kill Ramirez. She would not last long once she made her move, but at least she had been patient so far, waiting for the right time.

She often slept in his tent to avoid the other men, but since it was wide and roomy she had made her own space and he was not allowed to intrude. Sometimes he brooded in the night, looking at her sleeping form, wondering what would happen if he climbed in beside her and took her in his arms. Then he realized that this would make him as bad as the men who had attacked her before, for he was not sure if he could control himself once he started. Knowing her was frustrating indeed.

After a week the word came from Brogan that Ramirez wanted to see his three new men. Once more they were in the building where barely any light was allowed. Ramirez was shouting when they came to the door with Brogan, and they could hear the calm voice of Justine reasoning with him, calming him down. Brogan announced his arrival and went in by himself. It was clear that the leader was now raving against those who would work against him; no one else would be allowed to see him in this state.

Finally Brogan allowed them to come in. Ramirez was pacing up and down. He looked at them with red-rimmed eyes. Even in the dim light of the room Flint could see that the skin on his forehead was breaking out, worse than before, with tiny oozing cracks on the surface weeping pus in different places. Justine was in the background as before. She flashed the three of them a warning look with her dark eyes. They would have to watch what they were saying. Brogan stood to one side, ready to jump in when he was needed.

'They're out to get me,' Ramirez said. 'You are my best fighters now. You will have to get them.'

'Who's out to get you?' asked Ty reasonably.

'Enemies.' Ramirez stopped pacing and thrust his face forward into Ty's. 'Don't you understand? A successful man like me has enemies who want to get him?'

'We've received a warning,' said Brogan.

'A lone rider, one of my men, who was in one of the three towns, discovered that ten strangers were staying there, all looking to come into the hills.' said Ramirez.

'What, looking for minerals?' asked Flint. It was the wrong thing to say.

'They're looking for minerals all right Gold – the gold of the revolution,' spat Ramirez.

'If we're going to do this right,' said Brogan, 'we'll need to take up defensive positions outside as well as inside the fort. That's where you three come in. You'll be armed with guns and rifles. When they come charging in you'll hear a signal from the Point. Then you stop them.'

'You've got plenty of fighters. Why us?'

Ramirez stopped his restless pacing and stared at Flint.

'You are trying to play games with me? Didn't you notice?'

'Notice what?'

'I've sent a dozen of my best men out in the last week to do my work in other states. You three are some of the best fighters I have left.'

Flint knew immediately what this meant: the others had been sent out on the business of holding up trains, robbing banks and stores. Ramirez had been working up to one last big push to get the money he needed. He seemed obsessed by this to such an extent that he had forgotten what he had told them at their first meeting. He stood and looked at them; there was a dry stillness about him.

'Not only are my best men out doing their work, but I've had to have four others killed.'

'Why?'

'They decided they were here to make a profit and they were tired of waiting. Brogan brought them to me one by one.' He picked up the knife from his desk, the skull head glinted in what little light was allowed to filter through the drapes. 'I did what was necessary. They think that, because of this,' he indicated the skin on his forehead and face, 'I am helpless. But I walk in the night too. I look and I listen to what is being said.'

He smiled in a way that made their skin creep. 'I made sure that they did not die pleasantly or quickly. There was surprisingly little blood, but that did not matter, for they would rather have seen their life blood spill before their fading eyes and their lives end quickly than endure my methods.'

Brogan kept a stiff face, but it was clear that he was not particularly happy about what he had seen taking place in that room. Justine was there, her features standing out in the dark background, her slightly parted lips the colour of dark blood. She too had a look that combined a warning with horror at what she had seen.

'Now that you understand where we are, gentlemen, I want you to take the weapons, man the positions you are given. Do what ees necessary to kill these men. You will not fail.'

As they left the room Flint found that he was shivering even though the air around him was not cold.

As they went out into the bright sunshine, blinking as their eyes adjusted to the light, a wagon rattled through the open gate. On the back of the wagon, wrapped up in a net, tied with thick rope to the rail at the sides, was a snarling, growling thing. Beside the cart trotted four big mongrels, tails up, noses in the air, who answered its growls with their own. For a moment Flint thought he was imagining things, for the creature was four times as big as a man. The driver of the wagon, a big man called Jacob, smirked at them.

'Look what we got. Captured it on the lower slopes. Brought it back here fer Ramirez.'

'He sent you out to capture a bear?' asked Flint.

'Naw, son, he didn't, but if there's a bear in the offing an' we can get it, we do.'

'Why?'

'Gives the men a bit of sport. Bear-baiting they calls it. Stops 'em from being bored up here. The ladies like it too; gets 'em going.'

The two men at the front of the wagon got off, while help came running. Together they carefully pulled the snarling bear, still wrapped in the net, on to the ground, grabbed ropes attached to the net, then pulled the bear to the pit in to which it fell in with a dull thump, still rending the air with blood-curdling noises. The dogs circled around, whining with excitement, but were careful not to fall in. One of the men took out a sword and cut the circling rope that held the net tight, freeing the captive animal. The net was pulled away from the pit to be reused another time.

The bear stood on its hind legs, the head just below the top of the pit. It gave vent to more low growls and howls, pawing at the dogs and men.

'Tell you something else,' said Jacob. 'Once we're finished with it, there's some mighty good eatin' in that thing. You can't beat a good bear steak. Sure beats horsemeat. You can turn the hide into the best fur coat you've ever worn. Ramirez is goin' to be pleased.'

'While you've been out there wasting time we're been facing a situation here,' said Brogan.

'What?'

Brogan explained and curtly ordered the men into their positions to defend the fort. He took Flint and his companions to the weapon store. They were issued with Winchester repeating rifles, Colt army pistols and a stock of ammunition for both. They went to the corral, where they selected their respective mounts, Flint managing to regain his own horse. He would trust the sturdy animal on any terrain, and fighting on a series of crumbling hillsides was not going to be easy.

He could see from the looks being given to him by both Ty and Matt that they were expecting some kind of leadership from him. Brogan had stayed inside the fort. They were now on their own. Flint rode up to the other two once they were far enough from the walls for their conversation not to be overheard.

'I want out of this,' said Matt immediately. 'I say we just

take these weapons and go.'

'You don't want to be rich for the rest of your life?' asked Flint.

'You keep saying that, but nothing ever happens.'

'We need some kind of break, the right information,' said Flint. 'But before that, I say we get into good cover. We'll keep our horses with us, but dismount and part from each other in front of the fort. The trail spreads out before this area, so we're more likely to catch them lower down near Dead Man's Rock.'

'Wouldn't it make more sense for us to go to where the trail narrows down there and pick them off one by one?' asked Ty.

'Surely would,' said Flint, 'but I guess you haven't cottoned on yet to what's happening.'

'What?'

'Brogan and Ramirez want to keep us in line of sight of the fort. They don't trust us that much. Sure as eggs is eggs, if we took off he'd be out here to shoot us down faster than a cat off a hot skillet.'

'They are right not to,' said Matt. 'If I could get out of this now I would.'

'Now listen, Matt, hold your fire as long as you can, until these men are right on top of us,' said Flint.

They took their horses down to the lower slopes of the hill where the sturdy, low bursages and acacia bushes provided enough cover to keep them out of sight yet gave them a good view of the way the marauders were coming. Flint just had time to wonder why anyone would attempt to attack Ramirez in the first place, when the horsemen appeared. They numbered ten in all, as he had been told. They were big, purposeful-looking men, who wore bandannas over their faces probably more for protection against the dust and flies than to conceal their features.

Flint noticed that their saddlebags were bulging with water, food and other accoutrements. They had various weapons sheathed at their sides for ready use. Flint had warned the other two not to make a move before he fired his first shot. He was waiting until their leader, who wore a poncho and a wide-brimmed hat, was almost level with him, ready to be shot off his sturdy mustang, when something stayed his hand.

The leader brought his men to a halt. They were in a dip in the hills just below the eye line of the fort. He held up his left hand and indicated that they should go in that direction, away from the fort itself. Then they turned their horses and began to ride in a line that would take them out at the Point, or close to it. From this Flint concluded that they were not interested in old Fort Lincoln at all. Curious, he waited until he saw where they were heading.

'Nearly there, amigos,' said the leader. 'Get ready to take out the observer at the Point. Then we can get our mission done before they get us.' He had a tinge of Spanish in his accent. One of his men nodded and took out a Winchester rifle.

This was not an attack at all. It was a mission by men who wanted something badly and were prepared to fight for it. The truth was, if those in the fort had not been prepared they would have never have known that the riders were there at all, because they were keeping themselves at a level that allowed them to remain unobserved from the main building.

Flint decided it was time for them to carry out their attack. He fired at the man with the rifle. The man gave a scream and fell off his horse, wounded. The others did not wait to give their companion any help, but spurred their horses into action and rode off in the direction of the hills to the right of the fort. Flint mounted his own horse and chased after them. As they passed Ty and Matt, those two jumped up from where they had been concealed and let loose, wounding another two men. Flint was not interested in any of them; he was after the one who was their obvious leader. Besides, the other riders were suddenly besieged because a loose cannon shot came from the fort, where those within had been listening to the rifle fire. The ball came whistling through the air and landed inbetween the horses, causing them to wheel around in panic and knocking one or two of them to the ground.

The men dismounted and regrouped. They would have fired on Matt and Ty, who were separated from them by mere yards, but then there was another distraction. Brogan had obviously decided that it was time for him to get in on the action. He appeared, along with the bear-baiters, further up the slope. None of them were mounted; instead, what they did was to fling themselves flat on various bits of the rise in front of the fort and fire downwards at the so-called raiders.

Anyone who has been in this position knows it is easy to target downwards and harder to do so upwards. The men spread out so that they presented a wider target, but even so three of them went down almost immediately. Matt and Ty took no further part in the fighting because two of the men managed to remount their steeds and gallop after their leader, while another two were shot dead as they tried to do the same. The last two ran desperately up the slope in a last-ditch attempt to get those who had been gunning down their companions.

One managed to take out two of the bear-baiters, then there was the sharp crack of a Remington rifle and he fell backwards on the slope, a gaping wound in his chest as he tumbled over and over until he lay lifeless on the lower slopes. The last man faced Brogan, who had run out of bullets. Brogan launched himself at the man's feet, taking them out from under him, and then smashed the man's head against the rocky ground until the intruder was dead, his brains oozing out of his smashed skull on to the rocks.

In the meantime Flint was after the obvious leader, who was heading for the area of the Point. Flint found he was also being pursued by another two riders. They were some distance from the fort by now, high up in the rocky hills that folded so effortlessly into one another, where it was quite easy to hide or lose track of another rider.

The man in the lead obviously knew what he was doing, because he turned and fired almost casually upon the sentry on the Point with his rifle. There was a scream and the sentinel went down. Then the rider heeled his horse around and drew upon Flint, who already had a gun in his hand. The man did not seem to be afraid, and for the moment it was just the two of them, their horses having carried them forward at a pace that was dangerous in these rocky surroundings.

'Don't shoot,' said the man. 'I will offer you a treasure beyond your dreams if you come with me.'

'What?' They were far enough apart for Flint to have to shout to the man.

'I am Zack Mendoza. I used to be the second in command. I wanted none of this. I did not come here for war, just gold. Let me go and I'll come back again, and show you the way to get the gold.'

The fact was that Flint was so unmanned by this appeal that he hesitated.

'I don't know who you really are.'

'Then ask that evil hulk, the man who took my job, who told lies about me. Maybe he can give you answers.'

For a second Flint considered letting the man go because it was obvious that he was telling some version of the truth. He was just considering this step when they both heard the pounding of horses' hoofs and the other two invaders arrived.

'Kill him,' screamed Mendoza, making it obvious that he had just been stalling for time. Flint cursed himself for being a fool even as one of the riders took a pot shot at him. He spurred his horse forward, towards Mendoza, who had not been expecting that kind of move, and, using his right arm as a club, he hit the man hard on the side of the head. He wanted him alive. Taken by surprise, the leader gave a cry of pain and fell off his horse, landing with a bone-jarring thud upon the ground.

Flint heeled his horse round so that he was facing the other two. It seemed that with the unseating of their leader they were having second thoughts and were looking for a way of escaping, turning to head into the hills. Before they did so, one of them turned and aimed quite deliberately at Mendoza, who had staggered up from the ground, and shot him in the chest. The bullet felled him on the spot. Flint knew instantly what had happened. They did not want their former leader to be captured for the very good reason that he might reveal their names. To be wanted by the government is one thing, where they would at least face the possibility of being put on trial before imprisonment, but to be hunted by bandits was quite another matter. They would be shot dead on sight.

Flint let them go because he now had an object for his attentions. He did not know how long he had before Brogan would appear. He threw himself to the ground beside the dying man, who was breathing rapidly, eyes wide as he struggled to rise.

'You're a trickster, Mendoza. Don't let this go; you came here for a reason. Where is the gold?'

'Help me.'

'I'll do what I can. Now where is it?'

The dying man lifted his head and his eyes strayed towards the bluish mesa directly in front of the Point. Flint suddenly had a revelation. He knew now why there was a guard up there; it was nothing to do with the fort and everything to do with protecting the resources that belonged to Ramirez. He was guarding treasure, not people. None of the guards would have known the true nature of their posting. Mendoza gave a great guttering gasp and there was a dry rattling noise in his throat as he fell back on the ground, never to rise again.

Flint wasted no more time on the dead man. He went straight across to the man's horse and found something else in his saddlebags besides the usual dried beef, beans and water. He took out the sticks of dynamite and carefully concealed them under a rock beside an oddly shaped tree. Being out here in the hills had given him a good eye for locations.

He was just in time, because as he returned to the horses at the side of the corpse Ty and Matt appeared. coming between the hills and into the plain between the mesas. They came to a halt beside him and looked down at the dead man.

'You got him good,' said Matt. 'Did he fight real hard?'

'I didn't mean to get him killed,' said Flint. He was going to say that he hadn't meant for the raider to die at all, but managed to stop the words from coming out. He had a secret he was going to share with them, but not right now, since he could hear a further pounding of hoofs in the distance. 'I think someone lied to us about why these men were here,' said Flint. 'They wanted nothing to do with the fort, and they certainly weren't looking for a fight.'

'Then what were they here for?' asked Ty. Flint gave him a steady look and Landis understood at once what he meant by that unwavering gaze. 'You think so? So it does exist?'

Harper looked from one man to another, not quite understanding their meaning, but sensing it had something to do with their quest. Just as he looked at them Brogan came thundering through with three of his men, all he had been able muster when so many were out robbing for the cause. He got off his horse and examined the dead man before giving the corpse a hearty kick.

'Bastard!' He nodded to Flint. 'Well done, cowboy. Let's get rid of this stinking carcass, then tell Ramirez all's safe again – for now.'

CHAPTER TEN

Brogan was in a strangely elated mood as he looked at the dead man. Flint knew that it was because he had killed someone whom he, Brogan, had usurped, but since Brogan did not know that Flint had this knowledge, that young man decided not to point it out. The blood on the corpse soon coagulated in the hot air. The others expected Brogan to strip the body and throw it into a gully for the animals to eat, but he was more particular with this one.

'Load him on his horse; we're taking him in.'

Why Brogan would want to take a corpse back to the fort was a mystery to the new recruits, but they found out the answer soon enough when they got back to the command building. By this time it was late afternoon and the air was cooler up here in the hills. Indeed, in the winter it would get dark and the whole place could be covered in snow, such was the difference between being up here, several thousand feet above sea level, and down in the desert, even though the distance between them was just a few miles. Latitude was the crucial factor.

Brogan took the dead man past the pit in which lurked the bear (it had retreated into the covered part to get out of the sun, but still growled ferociously when anyone came near) and stopped in front of the administrative building. He rapped on the double front doors and for the first time since Flint had been there Ramirez came out of the building. He wore a wide-brimmed hat so that his face was in shadow, and had on a pair of spectacles with tinted glass to block out some of the still strong sunlight. On his hands he wore black gloves of soft, kid leather.

He stood there on the steps for a few seconds looking at the corpse, and then spat on it.

'We've met again at last, Mendoza,' he said. 'I should never have trusted you; you let me down all the time, keeping the proceeds that we needed to fund our cause. Then you came back here to try and take what was rightfully ours. You thought you could sneak in here by the back door, but I have eyes and ears everywhere.'

He looked over to his trusted aide. 'Take this one and throw him to the vultures with the rest. Take anything useful first.' He looked over at Flint and his companions.

'Good work; you have done well for the cause.' He nodded and went back into the building. Justine went behind him and carefully closed the doors. The audience was over.

The next couple of hours were spent disposing of the bodies. Landis, Harper and Flint were detailed with other men to do the job as quickly as possible. Wolves, bears, bobcats and other wild animals were known to roam these hills, so it was good policy to get the dead men away from the vicinity of the fort and dispose of them as far away as possible. One of the worst parts was when Flint had to climb up to the Point to get the sentry who had been killed by Mendoza. There was no way he could lift the corpse down, so had to throw the body over the side, hearing the sickening thud as it hit the ground forty feet below, the bones shattering as the dead man hit the ground.

While up there Flint looked towards the blue mesa that rose directly forward of where he was standing, his agile brain taking in the terrain. He lingered for a little too long and was shouted at to come down by the other men, who thought he had just been taking the opportunity to rest. They didn't know a thing.

In the meantime Brogan had been summoned to meet his mentor, Ramirez. The leader was looking well, the broken skin on his forehead had healed somewhat and although his features were covered in tiny scars they were not oozing as they once did. He was hatless now, sitting in an oxblood-coloured leather armchair that must once have been dragged up here to comfort the posterior of some two-star general who commanded this fort in the old days. The idea of someone having to drag such an object up here at great expense showed how little the army cared for its men in those days. As usual Justine was in the room, looking composed although her features were still pale.

'I have eaten well today,' said Ramirez. 'She prepares my food with her own hands and she takes care of me. Like you, she will be well rewarded when I am the ruler of this domain.'

'I think they were after what you have stored up,' said Brogan, a more practical man who did not like his boss to veer into what he regarded as these flights of fancy. 'They thought they could sneak in and take what was yours. Those new recruits did a good job too, especially that young man.'

'Then I think you should know what is going to happen,' said Ramirez. 'I have discussed the matter already with Justine, and I think it is time for our revolution.'

'The time is now,' agreed the girl.

'Wait a minute! We're seriously undermanned right now. I was pushed to deal with ten raiders and you're talking about a revolution!'

'The time is never right, in some ways, for such an event,' said Ramirez. 'How could it be so? What we do right now is plan so that when my men come back with our latest gains, we go and see the right people, me and you; protected by our men, of course.'

'What do you mean "the right people"?' asked Brogan.

'We have had this discussion, but of course we need to go over such things so that we do not make any mistakes.' Ramirez rose and looked at Justine. She handed him a sheaf of papers filled with beautiful copperplate handwriting.

'These are the people we need to contact. We will start meeting with them, one by one and convert them to our cause. Many are already sympathetic to the idea of being a breakaway state. You remember we discussed this many months ago?'

Brogan merely nodded at this.

'Well, we shall go forth now and do what is required.

Justine here will be my spokeswoman, for my unfortunate affliction sometimes makes people mistrust me.'

'I will be with you on your journeys,' said Justine. 'If we start now the revolution will begin in less than a year.'

'But you will need money, not treasure, to begin this.' Brogan passed a hand over his face.

'That has been taken care of too,' said Ramirez coldly. 'The money brought back here from our recent raids has been kept in this very building, under lock and key. You will have all the money you need.'

'So this has become a reality.' Brogan looked at the list again. 'A lot of people to see, a lot of palms to grease.'

'That is why we begin in just a few days. Do not forget, the other bandit chiefs are coming here to trade with me on this very matter.'

Brogan went to make immediate preparations for what he had to do. He mustered his finest clothes, knowing that his appearance had to be good, and he got one of the women whom he had been seeing for other purposes to make sure that his shoes were shined. He also went to the arsenal store and prepared his weapons. He was going to be seeing a wide variety of people. In his own mind there was no doubt that he was a fit man for the job. Like his brother he had plenty of chat and persuasive ability. Unlike his brother he was not a weak man, although inside him burned an attachment to gold. He also decided that the new men would be ideal for this mission – he would need at least six men with him.

As the evening wore on and twilight came on he went to seek out Jimez and Raul, his two loyal men, who had always done his bidding. He pretended he just wanted to eat with them but, like other men did, afterwards he went out for a walk and a smoke with them, drifting away from the main buildings, out through the main gate, then towards the back of the fort. The eating area itself was a place that he did not trust since conversations could easily be overheard by those who were passing back and forth. The tobacco was the finest gold flake they could get, stolen from a passing trader who had regretted ever meeting them. Brogan smoked one of his big Cuban cigars. He had a batch of these in his own quarters. He never shared these with his men, because he knew that rank has to show itself as superior. The three men leaned companionably against one of the walls near the very gap through which Flint had led his horse to warn the miners.

'Well, boys, I have a few things to say to you about Ramirez.' Brogan kept his voice low, a real effort on his part.

'What ees it?' asked Raul, his Spanish tones soft enough.

'The revolution has started,' said Brogan, 'and we are all going to be part of it. I can trust you boys not to say anything until this is official?'

'Of course,' said Raul. Jimez merely nodded his agreement.

'Good. Well the fact is we have to think a little about what we're going to do. Ramirez has a hell of a lot of money in the old command quarters. We can make our plans, get the key off him, take as much as we want and get out of here down the mountains. The down side of that is that he has a lot of men who are loyal to him, including those new ones.'

'Why don't you just go in and shoot him and the girl dead?' asked Raul. 'Then everything could be ours.'

'When the girl lets anyone in she promptly locks the door behind that person,' said Brogan. 'She also has a gun hidden somewhere in the folds of that long dress. Ramirez too is not defenceless. Because he isolates those who come in to see him – even me – it means that if he sees the slight-est attempt on his life he will strike first. I've never seen anyone so quick to react to a threat.'

'Just make sure you get in and stop the girl locking the door, and then we can rush in to his chamber, guns blazing,' said Raul. 'Don't give him a chance to defend himself.'

'Once more, I don't think that will happen. If we take that approach our raid will be heard and we will be sur-rounded within seconds. We'll be gunned down as soon as we leave the building.'

'Then what should we do?'

'I say that we pretend to go on the mission, but instead of greasing a few palms we go to where he hides his gold and take what we want before going over the border into Mexico, up the coast and into California.'

'Or we could just do as we're asked,' said Jimez, 'helping to create this revolution. It might be a fine thing, to help rule an independent country.'

'You could be right,' said Brogan thoughtfully. 'We would have money, position, power; if the revolution suc-ceeds we could do kind of well out of it.' The other two men perked up at the mention of these things. 'On the other hand, if it fails, we will be traitors with a price on our heads. We'll be hunted in every state. Which one would you rather choose?'

The others did not even have to think about what they were going to do.

'We're with you,' they said in unison.

'It's nearly dark.' Brogan threw away the remains of his cigar. 'Come on, let's get out of here.' The three men moved back towards the main gate.

Justine had decided to go for a walk that night. She often went out as the evening wore on, driven by restlessness that even she could not name. In her heart she was hoping she would see Flint so that they could talk at least, so that she could thank him for what he had done. Instead she saw Brogan and his two men drift towards the back of the fort. There was a crumbling area of wall near where she stood. She slipped through this and walked near the walls, slipping easily along, and invisible in her dark clothes. She did not like Brogan, had never liked the calculating way he looked at her.

She found herself at the back of the fort and, by standing near the gap, she heard him converse in that low, murmuring way. She struggled to hear his words.

They had a traitor in their midst.

It was a thoughtful woman who walked back home that night.

CHAPTER ELEVEN

Justine had a very restless night. She did not want to go up front to Ramirez and accuse Brogan of being a traitor. For a start, she knew it would lead to more bloodshed and she did not want that to happen within the fort. As far as she was concerned there had been more than enough killings within these walls.

The second reason had to do with Ramirez himself. She knew what his moods were like, he was not a man who would take the news that his supposed friends were traitors calmly. In fact he would be in such a rage that he very well might do himself a serious amount of damage. She knew that his moods affected his body. How this came about she did not know, but when he was calm and happy his skin condition eased and he became more comfortable, even though he could not take direct sunlight for long.

She had to admit that she wanted him to be well because she had feelings for him even though he was an evil man. At least, they said he was evil, and she had seen him do some terrible things. She had witnessed him torture men to death. But – and there was always the but – the men had tried to betray him. Ramirez was a thief, too, on a grand scale, but then again, he was a thief for a cause, thinking of only what he could do for the people. His need to help them was so great that he would create a new country. She decided, after barely sleeping, that there was only one person who could help.

She would go and see Flint.

She had been studiously avoiding him since discovering that he had moved a young slut, as Justine thought of her, into his tent. As far as she was concerned no blame attached to him: he was a man with the kind of needs normal men had. In a sense she could not blame the girl either. In a world as man-driven as this one a woman needed someone who could protect her, but she still harboured resentment against the girl.

She finally went to see Flint. She knew, as he and his companions did not, that soon the fort was going to receive a lot of visitors. Ramirez had managed to alert almost every outlaw in the country through his own secret network. The robbers, who were due to come back, were going to bring a lot of people of their own type with them.

The revolution had to start somewhere and this was how

it was going to be done: once they were paid, with a promise of a lot more to come, the men would go back to their own parts of the country and spread their insurrection. They would recruit others like themselves until one day those in power would find that the territory was now a country, and a country that they no longer ruled.

Brogan was going to put all that at risk.

Flint was in his tent when he arrived. Morven was away doing the things that women had to do to keep neat, tidy and feminine in a place like this. He was startled to see the pale features of the new arrival and backed away from her.

'Justine! It's an unexpected pleasure to see you here.'

'Maybe so. Are you going to be alone for a while?'

'I think so. Why?'

'I need to talk to you about Shaun Brogan.'

'What about him?'

'He's a traitor to the cause. He's in this just to get money. He's using Ramirez.'

'Hold on.' Flint studied her pale features. 'I thought that you were into a bit of betrayal of your own.'

'You mean this?' She moved her hands down the curves of her body. 'Nature gave me this body and it has needs. It is not a betrayal if it is used for what it is made for.'

'I don't know if your leader would see it that way,' said Flint ironically.

'This is why I chose you at the time, because you were a man with needs too.'

'Thanks. Good to feel wanted. Wait – you also sent me out to warn people on your behalf. Wasn't that an even bigger betrayal?'

'You don't understand. Those people were innocent. They did not need to be embroiled in the politics of this place.'

He accepted her explanation at once. Some would have found it hard to think that a woman so close to Ramirez would have some principles left, but he knew that people are neither black nor white, but different shades of grey. If he had relatives in Hope Springs would he not have warned them, too?

'All right, let's get down to business. How do you know that Brogan is a traitor?'

'Because I heard what he was saying and how he was saying it, too. He wanted Mendoza dead because inside he is just like him. There could not be two of them. At least Mendoza was trying to be underhand and take the treasure. The loss of the gold could have been borne, made up for in other ways, but what Brogan is doing strikes at the very heart of the revolution.'

'Why are you so passionate about this?' He studied her earnest face. 'What do you want me to do? In case you haven't noticed, I don't exactly have a great deal of power around here.'

'You have your own men. If you deputize them and take on Brogan I am sure you can provoke him in such a way that there is a showdown between you: your men and his. He likes to bully and command, I am sure he will rise to the bait. Will you do this thing for me?'

He did not know why, but something in him responded to her plea.

'I'll see what I can do.'

'Good, and Ramirez must think it is an honour killing, to preserve your rights. That way he will forgive you.' She came so close that her scent filled his nostrils. 'Goodbye, Flint. We will see each other in better circumstances.' She kissed him full on the lips, turned and went away. Seconds later Morven came in, looking back at Justine.

'What did she want?' demanded the girl.

'Nothing,' said Flint.

The next thing for him to do was to go and see Ty and Matt. They were sitting together at a fire between their tents, comfortably roasting some game they had taken earlier in the day. He looked around to make sure that no one else was able to overhear them.

'Boys, it looks as though we'd better make our move soon.'

'Why?' asked Landis.

'Because I've just found out that the old saw is true. There's no honour amongst thieves, and this place is going to blow wide apart, all thanks to that Brogan.'

'What happened?'

'I don't need to go into details. Let's just say that we've got to disarm the guard up at the Point, grab as much gold as we can and get out of here.'

'But they'll send a posse after us; we'll be as good as dead,' said Ty.

'That's why we've got to make our move the right way,' said Flint. 'Now, who's up for a fight with Brogan?'

'Time we did something,' said Landis.

'I guess so,' mumbled Matt.

'What's wrong?' asked Flint.

'It's us against all of them.'

'Matt, I'm worried too, but this is what we came here to do. Once Brogan's out of the way we'll make our plans, take what we need and leave.'

'Why provoke Brogan in the first place?'

'I made a promise,' said Flint, 'and I intend to keep it.'

He left the two of them mulling over what he had said. It was obvious that Matt was not happy with the idea of a showdown with the second in command.

'He's doing all this for that girl, don't you see?'

'Morven?'

'No, that Justine. She's been ready for him ever since he came here. You can tell by the way she looks at him.'

'Well, say he has a good reason for going along with her.'

'I s'ppse.' Matt got to his feet.

'Where are you going?'

'Don't know, just feeling restless, I guess.' Matt was a very physical man; when he was troubled by something in his life he would walk and think at the same time, it was as if the two things would go together.

'I'll come with you.' Ty rolled them a cigarette each and they strolled along through the grounds of the fort, not speaking to each other. Although they did not know it, this was to be when disaster struck.

'I just didn't want to be with you two after the killing,' said Matt. Landis looked around uneasily.

'Pipe down,' he said, 'we're not alone any more.' Indeed they were passing the mess hall, where some of the men were eating out on the stoop. What Ty hadn't figured out was that Matt, who was by no means vindictive or ill-natured, had to sort through things in his own mind, at his own pace. He ignored the injunction from his companion.

'It's just that when he killed Pete Brogan it made me real angry. Then you all explained that Brogan was taking advantage of me. Now he wants to fight again. Yet we never seem to get any nearer what we want.'

At that moment a hulk appeared in front of them flanked by his own two men. He had come around the corner of the building with them.

'Did I hear you mention my name? Who's killed someone called Brogan?'

'We were just speculatin',' said Ty.

'I heard the name Pete Brogan,' said the big man. 'I have a brother called Pete. What's happened to him?'

'I guess we'd heard of him too,' said Landis, attempting to save the situation.

'But he's dead?'

'Yep, we heard that, too.'

Brogan looked from one man to the other. Ty was looking him straight in the eye with a level gaze, but Matt was staring at the dusty ground, red in the face and confused by what he had done.

'Hey Matt, did you know Pete?' asked Brogan. The young man mumbled something about not knowing what Brogan was talking about, but addressing the dusty soil.

'You know, I heard a story that my brother had a good prizefighter working with him,' said Brogan. He was a man who had survived for a long time by being sensitive to what others were doing and how they acted towards him. 'I think your friend Flint met up with Pete and that there was a spat 'tween the two of them, and your Flint shot Pete dead. Is that right, Matt?'

Neither of the two men answered.

'Cover them, Raul, while I go and get this Flint. He'll be in the usual place. Bit of a loner, isn't he?' Brogan strode off with the other man.

Ty looked at Matt. Somehow he could not feel it in his heart to condemn him, but he had a feeling their treasure-seeking was over.

Flint was talking or, rather, arguing with Morven inside the tent when they heard heavy footsteps outside. They stopped the discussion instantly, knowing that this was the only way to preserving their lives, for they had been talking about her desire to kill Ramirez.

'Could I have a word with you?' asked Brogan. Flint was well prepared as he stepped outside, knowing somehow that he was going to be looking down the barrels of not one but two guns. He was. Jimez, also armed, stood beside Brogan.

'How can I help you two gentlemen?' he asked, 'Although it looks as if you've already made up your minds.'

'You killed my brother,' said Brogan, without any preliminaries.

'Matt,' said Flint instantly. He should have known it would come out one way or another if Mr Harper was involved. The man had a childlike desire to blurt out whatever was in his mind.

'You're coming with me to see Ramirez,' said Brogan.

Even before he had finished the words Flint sprang into action. He threw his knife and kicked the gun out of Jimez's hand so quickly that if you had blinked you would have missed the action. The knife was aimed at Brogan. The big man was surprisingly fast on his feet; he flung his body to one side, bullets pumping uselessly into the air where Flint had stood. The knife caught the big man on the shoulder, spinning him around. Flint jumped forward to pull it out and finish the job. He had not noticed that Jimez had dived to the ground and recovered his weapon. Just as Flint grasped the handle of the knife he felt a cold gun barrel in the small of his back.

'Leave him alone,' said Jimez.

Brogan dealt with his shoulder wound in a typical fashion. He left the knife embedded where it was because he knew quite well that there would be a torrent of blood when it was released, and he marched Flint across the parade ground of the fort to Ramirez's headquarters. On the way there Flint saw Ty and Matt, who were still being held at gunpoint.

'Let them go,' Brogan rasped. 'They ain't the ones I want.'

Ty was tempted to go for the shoot-out, because he still had his firing irons, but he knew that to do such a thing in the middle of the fort was as good as committing suicide. There was nothing he could do but join Morven, who was walking behind the prisoner and his escorts. She had dry eyes, and there was a look of determination about her that said that she was not about to give up hope for Flint.

Flint was marching steadily along, hands on his head as he had been instructed to do by Jimez. Matt and Ty walked further back, determined not to abandon their leader even in this extremity.

'Why are you taking him to Ramirez?' asked Raul. 'Why not just fill his stinking carcass full of lead?'

'Because he's Ramirez's bright-eyed boy,' grunted Brogan. 'I'm goin' to deal my side of the story 'fore he gets it for what he's done.'

When they got to the main block Brogan thumped briskly on the door with his left fist, wincing in pain as he did so. A few seconds later, after seeing what was going on, Justine allowed him to go in, with Flint in the lead.

'You try to make a move, the back of your head gets blown off,' said Brogan. He need not have worried. The prisoner had been completely passive since his capture. This was not to say that his agile mind had shut off, it was just clear to him that the more subdued things were right now, the better chance he had of survival.

Morven attempted to enter but Justine slammed the door in her face after telling them all to go away in tones that brooked no argument. Morven was very white-faced when this happened and the other two thought for a moment that she was going to explode with anger, but she kept herself in check. Along with her friends she did the only thing she could do: she waited.

Ramirez was waiting for them, stony-faced, as they brought his once golden boy before him.

'What happened? Why this?' His tones were quite mild.

'I've just found out about this miscreant idjit,' said Brogan. 'and because of it he attacked, tried to kill me. You can see for yourself.'

Ramirez stared at the knife that was still embedded in his second in command's shoulder.

'Certainly it was not his best attempt; if it had been me I would have got you straight in the heart.' As he said this he played with his own silver dagger, the skull on the handle seeming to laugh in silent mockery. 'But why make him a prisoner like this? If no one has been killed I order you to settle your differences right away. This is a good man, he has already been a great help in our cause. We need a man like this.'

'You say that, leader, but you do not know what he has done.'

'Has he betrayed me?'

'No, I haven't,' said Flint, speaking for the first time. 'This was a private quarrel between us.'

'Then you must settle your differences for the greater cause.'

'Do you believe in honour?' asked Brogan.

'Of course I do; it is what is making me take a stand, founding a new way.'

'Then you must know that this man, I have just found out, killed my brother.'

'Is this true?' The leader turned to Flint.

'Yes it is true,' said Flint evenly, 'but there was a reason. His brother tried to kill me first.' Yet inside his own mind he realized that he was being false in his reasoning. The fact was, he could have disabled the older Brogan without killing him. The man was a bluffing bully who would have crumbled at the slightest injury.

'My brother would not have tried to kill you without reason,' said Brogan. 'He was a practical man.'

'No more,' said Ramirez. He came right up to Flint and looked straight into his face with those hooded eyes and over-large pupils. 'You have tainted the honour of a family. I give this man permission to do whatever he wants with you to settle his honour.'

'No!' a cry of anguish escaped from the lips of Justine and she stepped forward. Ramirez quelled her with a single look.

Brogan used his good arm and propelled Flint across the room. Flint responded by crouching like a cat, ready for the fight. Brogan did not hesitate, but nodded to his two men. They managed to seize Flint in that confined space because there was nowhere for him to go, then Brogan carried out the one-handed beating.

He started by punching Flint on the head and the chest, and then punched him in the stomach. With each blow that landed on his face Flint whipped his head from side to side which lessened the impact of the blows, any one of which had the possibility of breaking his jaw. The punches to his gut did him an inadvertent favour as they made him sag forward. This made him harder to reach by a man who was already wounded. The other two were about to pull him upright when he gave a sudden jerk and freed himself from their grasp.

Flint leapt forward and was met by a punch in the face that knocked him against the men behind him, knocking one of them down. He was young and lithe, however; he rolled with the punch and sprang forward yet again. This time he stretched out for the knife embedded in Brogan's shoulder. His knife.

His questing fingers found the handle of the weapon. Brogan, seeing the danger, pulled back. Flint managed to knock the knife with his fingertips. Because Brogan had been moving his body the blade had already started working loose. Now the weapon clattered to the ground. The blood that had been stemmed for so long began to flow from the wound. If he wasn't attended to quickly, Brogan knew that he would lose a lot of his life blood, not a good idea in a place like this where if a man was weakened an infection could set in quickly and kill him.

Flint was about to pick up his weapon when he was grabbed again by the two men and held in a vicelike grip, They were going to make sure he would not get away from them again.

Justine quickly stepped forward, handing Brogan a cotton cloth; she always kept a store of such things handy in the room because of Ramirez's condition.

'Press this against your shoulder as hard as you can,' she said. 'Come with me, I have plenty of pads and bandages.' She did not explain that these too had been needed in the past by Ramirez. She picked up the fallen knife as she led the now dazed and blood-soaked man out of the room, because she needed a reference for the extent of the wound.

As Brogan was led out, glaring at his would-be victim, Ramirez, who had been standing at the back with his glittering eyes focused on the whole event, came forward.

109

'Perhaps he is right; perhaps you would have been a traitor to our cause. If you had the treachery to kill a man's brother, maybe you are unfit for us.'

'You are just a bunch of no-good crooks,' spat Flint.

'That may or not be so. We have a jail for those who behave badly according to our lights.' He rested his calm, reptilian gaze on the men holding Flint. 'Take him to the cells. Once Brogan has been treated and all is well, he shall be executed, but not until then. Take him away.'

Flint was dragged out past the astonished spectators and thrown into a lean-to jail with two cells at the back of the mess hall. The smiling jailers spat in his face as they locked him in, looking forward to his killing. It was evening by then, Flint knew that with the cold air and falling darkness they would wait until the morning to exact their revenge. He crawled under a thin blanket and nursed his wounds. Brogan had loosened a couple of teeth, his nose had been bleeding and he would have at least one huge black eye, but most of the damage was inside his head. He had failed.

His chance for gold was gone.

CHAPTER TWELVE

Morven wasted no time. When she saw that the door to the command quarters had been left open by the two men she rushed forward. This was her chance to get inside and wreak her revenge on the man who had caused her so much suffering. Luckily she was restrained by Matt and Ty.

'Do you really think that you'll do aught in there?' asked the Texan.

'I could try,' spat the girl.

Shortly afterwards one of the bandits appeared and sealed the building. They knew that their leader was under threat all the time and they were not going to take chances. For the moment it seemed that none of Flint's friends were being blamed for the events that had led up to his incarceration, or indeed for the death of Brogan's brother.

'I suggest that we get out of here,' said Ty.

'But it's getting towards night,' said Matt.

'I don't mean out of the fort. I mean to where we're billeted,' said Ty. 'We'll think about getting some supplies together and getting out of here as soon as we find out what's happening with Flint. Won't be long before they pick on us for associating with him.'

They made their way back by way of the jailhouse. It might have been a lean-to, but it was of sturdy construction and had only two small windows, one at the back and one at the side. It must have been where the army would have kept deserters, drunks or crooked soldiers. Morven was with them now; they had become her protectors in this place of mistrust.

There was a guard inside the prison, sent out there at Ramirez's command. Morven went to the back of the building.

'Flint, are you there?' she asked, her voice soft in case she attracted the attention of the guard. There was no answer so she called him again.

'Go away, there's nothing you can do.' Flint appeared at the barred window, his face bloodied and bruised.

'I'm sorry,' she began.

'Go away,' said Flint. He looked at her steadily. 'There's nothing you can do, none of you. Boys, look after her.' He turned his head. 'Now vamoose, the guard's coming.'

The girl left with the other two, not knowing what else she could do in the present situation. She was back at the tent she had once shared with Flint – why hadn't he tried to be with her in a physical sense? Then she heard a noise outside and Justine came in, her finger to her lips.

'Listen, I don't have much time. Ramirez thinks I'm still treating Brogan.'

'I hope that bastard dies!'

'Well, I stemmed the bleeding and bandaged him up. He's going to live, it was a clean cut. But I've got this for you.' She held up Flint's knife.

'Why didn't you give it to him?'

'If I try to talk to him the news will get back to Ramirez. He's insanely jealous, you know.'

'Why would you want to help us?'

'Just take the bloody knife!'

'How will I get it to him?' asked Morven as she took the weapon.

Justine looked at her. 'You're a woman,' she said drily. 'I'm sure you'll find a way.' Then she was gone.

Later that night. Morven went alone to the lean-to prison and tapped on the door. The guard inside was bored because he could only smoke and taunt the prisoner. Flint had been morose, answering taunts in monosyllables, so even that option gave limited satisfaction. At least a visitor would provide a diversion for a few minutes. The door was thrown open and the guard appeared, holding an oil lamp. He was a small, greasy man of Mexican extraction with large side whiskers, and was quite taken aback to see a young woman standing there. Morven had made sure that her appearance was more than acceptable and looked very trim and pretty.

'What is it you want, *señorita*?'

'*Buenos noches.* I come here because of your prisoner.'

'Why would that be?'

'We are lovers, he is a condemned man. I would see him one more time for that which he desires.' She fluttered her eyelids as she said this and the man got the message.

'Ah, *el amor*, the dance of love. Eet is not my job to let that happen, *señorita*.'

'After a suitable period of mourning, I can make it worth your while.' She smiled at him again. She wondered if he would really think that a woman who was mourning her dead lover would want to go near a horrible little man like him afterwards, but the human capacity for self-deceit is endless.

'Then you come in,' said the guard. 'I am Ramon.' He hung up the oil lamp and let her go inside. The interior of the building had a strong smell of stale sweat. Directly in front of the sturdy wooden chair in which the guard would sit were the two cells. They were not big, and were secured at the front by a line of iron bars with a built-in locked gate in each. Flint was in the left-hand cell. He was on the bunk, his face turned resolutely away from his guard. He did not stir when he heard her voice and was either asleep or feigning indifference.

There was a shotgun propped against the wall beside the chair, and for one wild moment she considered snatching this, but Ramon kept his body between her and the weapon.

She was wearing a long flowing dress that reached to her feet and Ramon looked at this disapprovingly.

'This ees no good, *señorita*, you might have a weapon on

you. There will have to be a search.'

She had no choice but to comply with his wishes. He was thorough in his search, taking the opportunity to lift her skirt, and lingering at bits of her anatomy where really no weapons would have been concealed. She resolved that if she ever had the chance her boot would linger on the most vulnerable part of his anatomy, propelled there with great force by the motion of her leg.

At last he proclaimed that he was satisfied and she was able to do what she had come here for. He picked up his shotgun and motioned for her to move towards the cell. She did not have to go far. Her head was almost touching the rough beams of the sloping roof. He waved her to one side while he put a key in the lock, then he opened the cell door and motioned for her to go inside. He turned the key again. Flint stirred and looked at her in astonishment. He really had been asleep.

'Ramon.' The girl looked at the guard.

'Yes?'

'This is going to be a delicate matter between a man and a woman. Will you give us a little privacy?'

'*Señorita*, consider it done.' A northerner might not have left them alone, but the Latin temperament understands the need for such things for, after all, what is life about beyond just eating and drinking and making money? The love of a woman is much of the rest.

'What the hell are you doing here?' Flint hissed at her. 'You'll get both us killed.'

'I couldn't leave you like this.' She kept her voice low and sweet, murmuring in his ear as if they were exchanging sweet words of love. This was for the benefit of the guard outside. The night was cold and nothing stirred except for the sound of the odd howling coyote in the distance.

'I have a present for you.' She reached down and took off her shoe. There, stuck to the side, was the long thin knife that he had used so much in his adventures. The light in here was dim, coming only through the bars, so she handed it to him, though with some caution.

'Justine gave it to me. The only place he didn't search was the side of my foot. I'm sorry, it's not much of a weapon.'

'But it's enough to give me some kind of hope.' He gazed at her oval features, which he could barely make out in the dim light. 'I was going to give up. I felt that nothing could save me, but now you're here.' He gripped her tightly and she could feel his heart thudding. She put her fingers delicately on his bruised features, then she wrapped her arms around him. Suddenly their unity became more than just an excuse for him to get his knife. They were together in a way that they should have been in at a much earlier time.

They had only a few minutes together, and then there was a knock and a discreet cough from Ramon. They drew apart and arranged themselves modestly, in time before the guard came in. By this time Flint had hidden his knife under the straw mattress on his bunk. Ramon held the shotgun steadily on them as he unlocked the cell door, holding it just wide enough for the girl to slip out before closing it and clicking the lock into place.

'You must go now *senorita*,' he said to the girl. 'Treasure what you have, for the next time you see your lover he will be dead.'

CHAPTER THIRTEEN

Early in the morning, when it was still that twilight period between light and dark, an observer might have seen the curious sight of men setting up a platform at the side of the pit in which dwelt the bear that had been captured earlier that week. The animal growled a little at this, but did not pay the humans much attention because they were leaving it alone – for now. The platform was made of wood, and was of sturdy construction about two feet high and five feet square. It was placed as close to the pit as possible and had steps placed in front so it could be mounted without effort.

After it had been put in place a chair was brought out of the main building. This was no ordinary chair, for it was a grotesque parody of a human skeleton made out of teak. The back was a carved wooden rack of ribs, the arms of the chair were made to resemble arm bones, the front legs of the chair looked like shinbones although the back was just plain. Atop the whole of this grim caricature was a wild, grinning skull that would glare out from above the head of anyone who sat there.

The suggestion of an impending show was completed by the erection of a three-sided tentlike structure on the platform, with the fourth open side facing the bear pit. Matt and Ty looked at this from a distance, only one of them puzzled by what was going on.

'I don't get it,' said Matt, scratching the side of his head.

'Don't you? Well, there's goin' to be a show, and I guess

I know who the main attraction is going to be.'

'Flint?'

'Give that man a coconut!'

'Can't we stop them?'

'Don't rightly think so. They didn't blame us, Matt, but we're his company. Can't do any harm to prepare, though, in case we can turn this to our advantage.'

'What way?'

'Well, they're going to be distracted; that's always a good thing. They'll all want to see this, which will make it easier for us to get away, maybe.'

At eight o' clock that morning, by which time most of the bandits were up and about their business, people began to drift towards the pit, called there by the message that had come from those who were still in the fort. Their leader wanted them. The sun was still low in the sky but the air was heating up already.

Most of those who manned the fort – except for lookouts – were assembled near the hole in the ground when Ramirez made his grand entrance. He walked out of the main door flanked by Justine and Brogan.

The latter was not looking his usual robust self, having lost a lot of blood the previous evening, but he was wearing his big fringed jacket to conceal the extent of the bandaging, and the look on his face was one of defiance.

Ramirez looked tall and stately. He wore a fresh white cotton shirt, blue jacket with intricate designs sewn on in gold, dark trousers and high boots of Spanish leather also patterned with hand-crafted designs. On his head he wore a dark hat with a curved brim, tilted to one side. He looked every inch the leader. Around his shoulders was a black cloak. Without a word he mounted the platform accompanied by

117

Justine and sat on the grotesque chair, the wooden skull grinning maniacally above his head. He now had the best seat in the house, because from his elevated position he could see every detail in the dug-out area below. Brogan chose not to climb up beside his leader, but instead took a position beside the platform, his back upright, looking the very image of a second in command.

The bear, aware of the crowd, was now pacing up and down in its pit on all fours, growling and whining in a low, anxious manner that did not bode well for anyone who might come into close proximity.

Matt, Ty and Morven were close to the platform, but none of them were close to the edge of the pit for the moment. The crowd was now about fifty strong. Most of them were not bandits, but those who kept the fort running: the cooks, the women, the horsemen and others with varyng skills.

Ramirez did not want to waste time. He was protected, for now, by the pale light of the early hour and the shelter of the structure within which he sat, but he had a limited time here and did not want to show any weakness to his people.

'You may wonder why I go to all this trouble? The sad thing is that people have taken advantage of my good nature,' said Ramirez softly, yet in a voice that carried to every one of those present. 'What you are about to see is an example of what happens to these who defy my authority and come here seeking the treasures put aside for our cause. Traitors will die. Go, get the prisoner.'

He addressed this remark to Raul and Jimez, who gave curt nods and went to the brig. The guard surrendered the prisoner to them and they escorted him across the parade ground of the fort. This was not made easy for Flint. He had been placed in leg irons and his hands had been tied behind his back by Jimez. He was not helped by the fact that one or the other was continually smiting him across the back as he walked, urging him to hurry up, making him stagger in his chains, raising clouds of dust and having precisely the opposite effect from that which was intended.

The spectators parted as he came closer so that he had easy access to the platform. Morven wanted to go to him, but she was restrained by Ty and Matt. Even Matt knew what Ramirez would have done to them if they dared to interrupt his spectacle.

Flint was a piteous sight, since the wounds he had received the day before had not been cleaned. His jaw was swollen, he had a huge bruise around his right eye, and his face was streaked with dried blood from an encrusted cut below his left eye.

He was taken to face their leader. He stood in front of him saying nothing, but holding his head up and straightening his body. If he had to die he was going to die like a man.

'Like all men you are entitled to a hearing,' said Ramirez. 'But you had that hearing yesterday and you attacked my best man. You are sentenced to death. Do you have anything to say?'

'Get on with it,' said Flint. He shook his head wearily. He had seen men die in various ways and he wanted to get on with his own death as quickly as possible. At least that way he would be at peace. However, he didn't really intend to die just yet because he had a concealed weapon that they did not know about.

'A brave man,' said Ramirez. 'Take off his bonds and let him meet the great hairy one.' The two followers unshackled Flint's legs and cut the ropes that bound his hands behind his back, then they turned him round to face what had now become a bear pit.

Many of the bandits and the servants in the crowd were exchanging money. It seemed that they were betting on how long he would survive the ordeal before his inevitable death. This did not increase his confidence one bit. Nor did the size of the creature he was facing.

In his cell, treasuring the memory of the visit from the woman who had become his lover, he had touched the knife once or twice. It was like being in the company of an old friend. In his head he had pictured his heroic fight with the bear, how he would rush in and stab it to the heart before it could attack him, how he would get away from the dying throes of the animal and how he would escape from there and take his revenge on those who had imprisoned him.

Now he was faced with the awful reality of what he was up against. He had forgotten how big even a young grizzly bear can be. Fully grown, this thing would have been nine feet tall on its hind legs, but even at seven feet it was still far taller than anyone there, and as broad as an adobe wall. When it paced around on all fours those huge forearms rippled with power. His imagination withered and died now that he was faced with the incomparable rawness of nature.

'Throw him in,' said Ramirez. 'May you die well, my friend.'

Flint was picked up on either side by the two Mexicans, then thrown bodily into the pit. As he flew over the edge Morven gave a scream of fear, starting forward, only to be restrained once more by Ty and Matt. On the platform Justine looked white-faced too, as she saw him being flung to his inevitable death.

For a moment he felt as if he was flying, then he landed

on the ground with a thud that should have knocked all the breath out his body. Fortunately he had prepared for the moment and instead of landing with a crash he relaxed and rolled over so that the impact was lessened. It was a trick he had learned from working with horses. Once or twice his steed had been shot out from under him and he had used the same technique to get away from the danger zone.

The crowd seemed to hold its breath as he fell into the pit, fully expecting him to be ripped to bits within seconds.

'Look,' someone shouted, 'he's got a knife!'

Flint was now crouched in the arena, the blade of his knife glinting in the sunlight as he waited for the confrontation.

This did not happen immediately because the bear, confused and annoyed by the shouts and screams of the humans, had retreated into the covered area, frightened by all the sudden attention. That was a situation that would not last for long; already Flint could hear it snuffling and growling as it sensed that there had been a change in its situation.

Flint looked around and saw something that no one else would have taken into account. There was a dismembered carcass of a dog lying to one side of the area. Much of it had been eaten. He knew immediately what must have happened. The animal would have been at the side of the pit, barking defiantly at the bear, when a critical misjudgement had made it fall over the side. This meant that the bear had eaten quite recently.

The grizzly emerged from the covered area into the light of day. As close up as this it looked huge. To the spectators Flint looked incredibly puny. His knife looked so useless it was laughable.

Flint looked around, then he did something that seemed to those watching to be incredibly stupid. He tucked his knife into his belt threw himself to the ground and lay still, apparently not even breathing. To those watching he seemed to have given up entirely. They began to boo and shout at the figure lying on the ground, with the word 'coward' being repeated over and over again. The bear lifted its head and sniffed the air, pawing and growling at those above. Then it ignored them and concentrated on this strange presence.

What those above did not know was that Flint had hunted bears in his youth; he knew their ways, what they would consider to be a threat. By throwing his body to the ground he had disarmed one of the bear's defence mechanisms. Like any other animal, when a bear sees a moving object it takes this as a threat. In addition, bears like fresh prey and tend not to eat animals that have already died and, to the bear, Flint was another dead animal, although one that was still warm. The bear did not take into account the fact that Flint had been crouching there just a minute before. Animals do not think in that kind of way.

The crowd were now getting furious with Flint, baying for his blood, some so close to the edge that they were in serious danger of slipping in. From his platform Ramirez watched the whole thing with an impassive look on his face. Que sera sera, that look seemed to say. Brogan took out his gun and toyed with the idea of shooting a bullet into the beast to stir it up to fury, but looked at his leader and thought better of the idea.

Flint waited there as if dead, judging the right moment. The bear sniffed his legs, then his back, then the back of his head. The hairs on his neck rose as he felt the hot breath of the animal on his neck and smelt its nauseating stench. The bear gave a growl of dissatisfaction and lumbered away. At this point Flint went into action. He prayed that his legs, so lately bound, would work as he asked them to. He got up. The animal now had its back to him but was still on all fours, lifting its blunt head to sniff and growl at the crowd.

When Flint got to his feet there was a swelling shout from the spectators who suddenly realized that their sport had not yet ended. But Flint did not pull out his knife and attempt to stab the beast in the neck. This would have been the worst thing to do considering the rolls of fat there. Except for a lucky blow to the brain-case the animal would have hardly felt a thing. Instead, Flint threw his body on to the back of the animal. He was atop the bear's furry hide, pulling his slim body along until he was level with its head.

Enraged by this daring act the bear responded by rearing up on its hind legs. The spectators started going wild as Flint grimly clung on to the animal, his only option at this point. Incensed by the intrusion of the puny one who had dared to assail its person, the bear stuck out its forelimbs, gave a roar that seemed to shake the earth around for yards, then rushed forward towards the spectators, evidently feeling that they had played some part in the matter.

This was the chance he had been waiting for.

Flint drew his body up even further, grabbing handfuls of fur and hide as he did so, pushed with his boots against the animal's shoulders and threw his body to the side of the pit. The crowd had drawn back when the bear came towards them. This gave him some leeway for movement. He hit the side of the pit with a rush that knocked most of the breath out of his body. His fingers scrabbled in the deep soil as he tried to obtain some leverage. He managed to draw his body forward so that he was half in and half out. If he failed now he would slide downwards and would be ripped to bits by the enraged animal.

Just as he was almost out the bear struck out with its claws and managed to snag the left leg of his trousers. The animal was scarcely hooked in the cloth but it was so strong that one jerk would be enough to pull Flint in. The claw hardly touched his leg, but still managed to score a trail in his flesh that would hurt later. Then he felt the cotton of his trousers give way and he was back up on his feet on the edge of the arena.

He was not out of danger yet. Brogan faced him across the gap, and was pulling a Colt out of his holster. Flint was faster. He took out his knife. It arced across the gap and embedded itself in Brogan's chest. Brogan dropped his pistol and looked down with an almost comical expression of surprise on his face. He pulled out the knife and looked at it stupidly as, for the second time in twenty-four hours his life blood blossomed as a stain on his front. The knife fell with a barely audible thud. Brogan staggered forward and fell eight feet to the ground.

The bear, cheated once of its prey, was not about to let this one get away. As Brogan staggered forward the animal took him it its terrible embrace.

'Noooooo,' Brogan, still alive, gave a terrible cry of fear and horror. Then there was a crunching noise that made even the most hardened men there wince in disgust and Brogan's head parted from his body as those terrible jaws crunched their way through the flesh, bone and gristle of his neck. Brogan's lifeless head rolled along the ground then came to rest with his dead eyes staring sightlessly up at his former leader.

For a second Brogan's body stood upright, blood spurting from the ragged remnants of his neck, then it crumpled to the ground, limbs still twitching.

Not that Ramirez was paying too much attention to the demise of his traitorous lieutenant. He jumped off his skeleton chair, took out his own knife mere seconds after Flint had thrown his own, and hurled it across the gap. Justine was at his side by then. The knife was aimed with deadly accuracy, but Flint was full of energy following his successful escape from the bear, and he threw himself to one side. The silver-handled knife embedded itself instead in the throat of the man standing behind him. The man gave a choking, gurgling sound and fell into the pit. He too was taken into the furry embrace of the grizzly and had his face bitten off.

Ramirez grabbed a gun from Justine, who had produced it at his command, and began to run around the large hole in the ground, pointing the weapon at Flint. At that moment Matt and Ty looked at each other. No one was taking them into account and this was possibly the one chance they would ever have to escape. Ty knocked the strange chair off the platform with a sweep of his hand, then ordered Matt to the other side. They heaved the platform into the pit. There was a crash as it landed on the deep, compacted soil, and the bear retreated, howling, frightened by this new intrusion.

However, bears are animals who know how to climb trees using their claws to gain leverage. This one sniffed at the platform, decided it was not going to do any harm, climbed atop the wooden structure. Then it reared its head above the pit and scrambled out, digging into the ground with claws that could dismember a man with one sweep, and dragging out its body by using those massive forearms.

In the meantime Ramirez had to turn and defend himself from a new attacker. Just as he was drawing a bead on Flint, a bullet zinged into the alkaline dust at his feet, causing him to jump back with a muttered '*diablo*,' while twisting round at the same to find out who his attacker was.

He found that he was facing a vengeful woman in the shape of Morven, who had managed to wrestle a gun from Ty. As Flint ran round, this time to defend her, Ramirez gave a cry of pure hatred and pointed his weapon at her head.

He did not have a chance to shoot. By this time the bear was out and not in the mood for playing. It ran towards the leader. Ramirez took one look and did what anyone with any sense would have done: he ran as fast as he could with Justine at his heels, knowing that a handgun would slow the bear down very little. They reached the nearby command house and retreated inside, slamming the door. The bear turned and ran towards the spectators, who by now had become a frightened, hysterical mob. Most of them were not professional bandits, they were the women, servants and cooks who ran the fort. Their presence blocked the efforts of the real criminals to deal with the bear. As it came back towards them, as though by an unspoken, mutual consent they turned and ran too, scattering in all directions.

Before this happened Matt ran with Ty, Morven and Flint towards the corral. A lot of equipment was kept there in a shelter so that the bandits could ride out at a moment's notice. A few men tried to block them as they went, but Matt lashed out with his formidable fists and soon the way was cleared. Most of those present paid them little attention as they tried to deal with the rampaging bear.

The horses were saddled up in short order. They had few weapons or supplies with them, but that made no difference. All four of them just wanted out of there; they could work out the rest later. Riding on, Flint heard the shooting start as sense prevailed and the animal was dealt with in the only way those inside the fort knew. He gave a silent prayer to Bruin, hoping that there was some kind of bear heaven for the animal that was supposed to have been his slayer but had turned out to be his saviour.

CHAPTER FOURTEEN

Once they were in the hills the others looked at Flint for leadership. It was still fairly early in the day, so the temperature was not yet too high for either them or their animals. Flint had managed to get his own horse, a fact which gave him a renewed sense of confidence.

'We keep down low at the tree line,' he said, 'and work our way behind those blue hills. Then we go to Hope Springs.'

'But no one lives there,' said Ty. 'We got them to clear out, remember?'

'Exactly,' said Flint.

Riding below the area where the trees gave way to low bushes and scrubland, the only vegetation the rocky soil could support higher up, was a sensible decision to take. This way they were able to ride their horses between the trees, avoiding being spotted by the man on lookout. The risk came from the fact that they were going through unknown country and might encounter other dangers they had not anticipated, such as slips, rills and dips that would be impossible to circumvent.

They also faced another danger. If Ramirez got his men together soon enough he would be able to follow them using one of his scouts. They could only hope that the disruption of that morning – not mention losing Brogan – would throw him off their trail for a while.

The bandits had not foreseen the kind of man they would be dealing with. Ramirez looked at the dead bear sprawled in front of the main block.

'Have that skinned, cure the hide. Cut up the meat and feed me bear steak tonight,' he ordered his men. He turned to Justine. 'How good are you at keeping the sun from me?'

'I can only do so much.'

'Do your best.'

'Why?'

'Because this is a matter of honour. My honour! They will die by no other hand than mine. Now do what you can to prepare me.'

The horses did well and they were on the far side of hill upon which stood the fort, still amongst the trees. Flint considered their position.

'If we go up here this will take us to the back of the hill facing the lookout post, then we can ride round and get to where we want to go. But first we stop for food.'

The others did not see the sense in this, but Flint knew what he was talking about. At first Morven was a little sceptical about what they could do from that angle, since they had only their horses and what they had been carrying at the time of their escape, but Flint soon trapped a couple of small animals and created a fire using traditional methods. He also made the fire low, using chips of wood so that there was very little smoke but it burned hot enough to cook the meat. While they ate, the horses cropped the tender shoots of grass that grew in the gaps between the trees.

When they had finished Flint put out the fire and covered it in soil so that even an experienced tracker would have found it hard to note that they had been there.

By this time they were on the far side of the hills overlooking the Point. It was time for them to get between the hills, so that they would be able to ride out to their intended campsite before they were tracked down.

Matt, Landis and Morven had been opposed to stopping for a rest, but now they saw the sense in Flint's decisions. By the time their horses had picked their way up to the base of the blue hills and they had started riding towards Hope Springs, some fatigue was already setting in. If they had gone there straight away they would all have been exhausted, including the animals. This way they at least had some chance of getting to their destination.

None of them said so, but there was some hope that the original settlers would have returned and would offer them help. They rode hard, so that by the time they reached the settlement they were getting tired. Flint, in particular was not in good shape. He had been beaten quite severely the previous day. His back and shoulders hurt, face was sore, and as he grew more tired his vision blurred and his head ached badly. There was a wound in his leg where the bear's claw had hardly touched him, but it had caused a score in his flesh and he was bleeding. He slid off his horse and had to steady himself against the animal or he would have fallen. Morven came to his side and steadied him too, her expression one of concern. She voiced no sympathy, however, knowing that she would just displease him.

The sight in front of them was one of loss and decay. Those who had come here with high hopes had obviously decided that, in the face of criminality, they were going to leave. One or two of the shacks were still standing, but most of the canvas dwellings were gone. A couple of old carts lay forlornly on the path that had once weaved between the buildings, but the only living things about the place were the birds who pecked at whatever remains they could find, and the rats who were never far from any kind of human habitation. Morven looked at this wreckage with dismay. She had pictured some little thriving community, not this desolation.

'What are we going to do?' she asked in despair.

'Hide,' said Flint.

'Where?' she asked looking around at the wrecked village.

Ramirez was dressed in his riding clothes: a red shirt, a loose coat of light cotton that hung around his shoulders, and black trousers tucked into his long, ornately patterned riding boots. He was also wearing a wide-brimmed hat made of lightly woven fibres. Most bizarrely of all he wore a mask of white damask that had been especially made for him by Justine, with holes cut for eyes and mouth, and with a drawstring at the bottom to pull it in so that it could be worn close to his features but not so tight that it would rub his skin. He marched out into the daylight like this, his hands encased in black gloves, a Colt .44 in each holster, towards the horse that had already been prepared for his use.

He looked around at the men who were there. They did not number a great many. The numbers would have been greatly swelled if he had waited for the other bandits to arrive, whom he had summoned to help start his revolution. But although he had only seven men, that was enough for him to take care of what had become personal business. Although the lookout in the Point had seen nothing, that did not deter Ramirez. He was dealing with men who knew what they were doing when it came to making themselves invisible, since they had been doing so for years with regard to the authorities. Ramirez knew this area like none of the men whom he employed. Sitting on his mount, with Justine at his side as ever, he looked thoughtfully into the distance.

'If you could not see them, they could have gone into town, in which case they will still be on the trail,' he said to the watchman, who had descended from his lofty viewpoint to speak to his leader.

'I didn't see them at all,' said the man. 'But them peaks make sure I can't see everything.'

'Then they were in the trees.' Ramirez pondered this for a while. 'They would want to go into town because they have no supplies, but maybe they also remained in this area.'

'But why?' asked Justine.

'They're after me,' said Ramirez, 'in which case following them might be a bad idea. I could be walking into an ambush.'

'I don't think that's right,' said Jimez, one of the accompanying men. 'After the rampage they escaped, pure and simple. They didn't have a thing with them.'

'Right, you men, come with me.'

Ramirez took his band of men into the hills beyond the point that could be seen by the lookout. Shortly after that he picked up on the trail left by Flint and his companions, the marks of hoofs still fresh in the ground.

They had taken over an hour to get to this point. Ramirez spurred his horse into action. He could not confess weakness to his men, but he had only a limited time to get this done because of his skin condition. Even now he could feel the heat of the sun on him. Up here in the hills it would only get worse.

They soon came to the deserted mining village. They looked around, finding nothing but wreckage. The ground here was stony compared to that near the fort, so they found only the occasional hoofprint.

'They must have left,' said Jimez.

'I am not so sure,' answered his leader. 'Let us look around.' He cursed in fluent Spanish as they found nothing except the entrance to the deserted mine workings a few hundred feet from the wrecked village. 'They could be in there,' he said thoughtfully.

'Shall I send men in with lighted torches?' asked Jimez, looking as if he really didn't want the job.

'No, I have a better idea.'

Ramirez had the horsemen gather around the entrance to the cave and handed them sticks of dynamite he had brought from the weapons store. They lit them at his orders, threw them at the same time and then rode off as hard as they could.

They gathered their horses as the explosion rent the air with an ear-splitting boom, followed by a loud rumble as the entrance, which had been shored up by wooden beams, collapsed inwards. Where there had been a regular way carved into the side of the hill there was now a pile of rubble made up of many large and small rocks all shifting together in the aftermath of the explosion.

Ramirez did not waste much time looking at his handiwork.

'Ride on,' he said, 'it's settled.'

Only Justine looked back as they rode away, her face showing some sign of sorrow for the man who had helped her not so long before.

CHAPTER FIFTEEN

The bandits had been right. The mine extended for hundreds of feet, sloping down as it went, with several passages leading off to either side of the main one. Flint had asked his companions to go in because he knew that they could be pursued for ever through the hills and his wounds would not permit him to go much further. He was so physically exhausted that the others had to half-carry him into the mine, along with some blankets and food that they had managed to find in the deserted camp.

They had followed his instructions with regard to the horses, tethering them to a spot where there grew a clump of wild bushes in a dip in the hills about half a mile before the camp. If they were careful the bandits would ride past this on their way to the camp. By the time they had done this and returned they too were feeling weak.

Ty was in a rebellious mood. He went down into the mine, where they were burning the torches left by the miners for light, using them one at a time. They had gone down about halfway before taking one of the branching passages at Flint's instruction.

'I reckon we should go out there and brass it out with 'em.'

By this time Flint was sitting against a rough rocky wall with his legs spread out before him. Despite being exhausted he was still very much in command of his thoughts.

'They would love that, you and Matt out there blasting away at them. They would kill you then come in for Morven and me. I would shoot at them too, but I'm a sitting duck here.'

'They might come down anyway.'

'Let them. With you two here in this side passage they'll spend all day looking for us if we don't bring any attention to ourselves.'

Of course, things were not so simple. That was when they heard distant voices echoing at the head of the mine, and they all fell silent, just glad that they had come back here in time. In the light of the smoky wooden torch Matt and Ty positioned themselves so that they could take out anyone who might be spoiling for a fight. The off-branch they were in rose upwards in relation the other branches. Matt had wondered loudly why Flint had brought them here when they would be safer further down.

For those in the mine the relief of hearing the voices fade away was soon tempered by the explosion that rocked the mine. They all heard the roof collapsing further up at the entrance. The tremors reached deep into the ground, with earth and debris falling on top them from the low roof.

'Cover your heads,' shouted Flint, holding his arms over his own.

Luckily this side passage had been shored up by some thoughtful miners and when the tremors subsided everyone was covered in dirt but otherwise unharmed. Ty gave Flint a grim look, took the torch and went exploring. He was so tall that he had to bend at the knees to walk into the main mine. He came back seconds later and the grim look on his face had intensified.

'What is it?' asked Morven, clasping her hands together.

'Hell, they thought we'd be here. We're sealed in.' said Ty.

Morven put her face into her hands and began to weep.

'We're all going to die!' yelled Matt, dislodging some more earth from above, so loud was his voice. He sputtered as the dust fell in to his mouth. Flint gave him a steely glare.

'Stop that. None of us are going to die.'

'We sure as hell can't dig our way out,' said Ty, 'not with our bare hands. Flint, we're done for.'

'Ty, don't put that head of yours too near some hot coals or a spark might set it alight. You dunderhead, don't you notice the breeze?'

Ty gave Flint a dumbfounded look while Morven stopped weeping, lifting her face out of her hands, and Matt stared at the three of them.

'You mean there's a way out of here?'

'Not so much a way, but air vents to keep the place fresh. See, when a mine gets too deep the air starts to get stale, so now and then they open a vent in the side of the hill.'

'What do we do?'

'We wait, that's what. I guess those bastards won't hang around too long when they think they've got what they want, but we'll wait, just to be on the safe side.' Now that they knew he had given them some way out of the mess they did as he asked and waited, talking in low voices about what they would do once they got out, for survival alone.

After about an hour of this they decided it was time to make their move. Flint had recovered enough to go with them as they went along the increasingly narrow tunnel. Soon they were in single file, with Morven in the lead holding the torch because she was the smallest and could walk almost upright. Ty was like a half-shut knife and Matt had to bend his broad shoulders.

'Look,' Morven said excitedly, 'the flame is flickering

towards me.' She went forward and found a hole in the side of the hill through which came welcome daylight and did indeed let in clear air. The hole was only a couple of feet wide, but by using the spare torches as clubs they were able to knock off some of the stones and dirt to widen it. Ty refused to let Morven go through first. He wriggled into the gap and found himself in a cavern about the size of a small house, with a narrow mouth that opened up to the side of the hill. He looked out cautiously and found they were on a slope overlooking the camp, but at such an angle that the entrance would have been invisible to those raiding the village.

The others came through, helping Flint, who looked around thoughtfully. 'Guess we get some salvage from the mining camp, including food if any, and we stay right here. We can block up the entrance at night, then in the morning we start building a more permanent place to stay.'

'All right,' said Matt. They were all too tired to argue.

Less than an hour later they had secured their makeshift home. Luckily they found more blankets and some dried food in one of the ruined shacks. They managed to catch some game, then lit a low fire inside the cave, putting up with the smoke for the sake of cooking their food and remaining invisible to the outside world.

'We can get out of here soon, ride for help,' said Ty, once they were fed.

'No we can't,' said Flint.

'Why not?'

'We have a job to do.'

A day or so passed at old Fort Lincoln. Ramirez had his bear steaks, enjoying them because they were the essence of the power that had been in the bear. Justine did not refuse to dine with him, but she picked at her food. They were dining together in the blockhouse, sitting at an oak table that had been brought here for the officers who had commanded the fort.

'Now they are gone things are going well,' he said. 'Brogan was a sad loss, but he was only a man and I have others to replace him.'

'That's good,' she said mechanically.

'I sense a lack of enthusiasm in you, which is understandable; you have been through much. The good news is, the other chiefs will soon arrive with their men. I have had scouts arrive who have told me they will be here in hours. It will not be long before the great work can begin.'

'You lost some good people who could have helped you.'

'That is life.' He shrugged. He watched as she pushed her plate away.

'May I be excused?'

'Of course, you look pale, tired. I am almost finished my repast.' He snapped his fingers and an obsequious servant appeared. 'Take these plates away. Pour me another wine. Then I shall go and greet those who will help me begin the revolution.'

Justine fled from the room. He could have sworn he heard a strangled sob, but perhaps he had been mistaken. He drank his wine in grand isolation, his thoughts already elsewhere.

Flint had been more badly wounded than any of them had realized. His leg had been scratched by the bear when they were still in the fort and he had not told them about this while they were on their journey or while resting. It was only when he groaned as he was trying to move his leg that

Morven found out what was wrong. Luckily there was a stream near by and she was able to wash and clean out the wound.

Unfortunately the dirt had caused an infection to set in and they remained in the cabin while Flint developed a fever. Luckily Ty always carried a flask of whiskey for an odd sip; loath though he was to give this up they used it to sterilize the wound.

Flint lay on his blankets for three days, soaked in his own sweat. Morven changed his bedding when she could, but the most important thing she did was to give him water, making him drink even when he was delirious. They all expected him to die. They had all seen the same kind of thing happen out here before, where even a minor scratch could turn into a deep infection that became septic, carrying the victim off in days. Survival was a matter of luck. Flint was young, he was lucky.

On the fourth day, swaddled in his blankets, when he had been so quiet in the early hours that Morven was sure of his passing, Flint spoke quietly:

'Where am I?'

Morven, who was hollow-eyed with lack of sleep, and a little gaunt too, came to his side.

'Flint, I thought . . .'

'What?'

'Never mind.' As he struggled to sit up she put her arms around him and helped him to rest against the rough wall of the cavern.

'I'm hungry,' he said. 'Do you have any stew?' The words sang in her ears as she prepared him food and drink.

At the fort Ramirez now had over a hundred men. Some of them were his own, but many were from the surrounding territories. They were all set for a war with the authorities. They knew it would not be easy, but once they had been primed with the correct details of what was wanted, they would go around the state causing insurrection at every turn. There is no honour amongst thieves, it is said, but many of them showed a deep respect for Ramirez. He had united them in a way that no other chief had been able to do. He stood before them as they gathered in their often rough clothing, with assorted weaponry in their hands, the day after they had come to receive their instructions. It was morning, not a good time of day for men such as these, but there was no doubting his magnetism.

'You think that you are successful at what you do? Well, the truth is, many of you are good, even great at taking the things you want. But the truth also is that none of you are as rich as you should be despite the work you have done over the years.'

There was a general nod of assent at what to them was a self-evident truth. He was manipulating them, a fact which many recognized, but he was appealing to their deepest instincts.

'The fact is, my friends,' he continued, 'that you have been separate, not together. Now you stand with me in a cause that will make many, if not all of you wealthy men. But that is not the only factor in this gathering together of the finest men that we can muster; you are all leaders in your own right who have come here because you know the power that comes from our becoming united.

'Once we spread our message and influence you will have your own territories, your own power. You will command not dozens, but thousands of people. We can do this thing. We can spread our influence through the revolution. We can, and we will win together! Who is with me?'

A rumble went through the men who filled the area in front of him as he used the wide steps of the main building as his platform, with Justine beside him. He stood and waited for what he wanted, knowing that it would come. The rumble turned into a groundswell, and then a roar as men shouted together in their assent for what he was asking. Some even fired bullets into the air as they roared their support for this man who would give them even more than they had dreamed of.

The revolution was beginning.

At the former mining village things had become a lot better. There was a stream that trickled down from the surrounding hills so that they had no shortage of water. Larger game was not hugely plentiful up here but they had plenty of birds and rabbits to provide their basic fare. Flint had a knowledge of which plants they were able to eat to supplement their meat diet. In addition, while Flint was ill Ty and Matt had gone and fetched their horses, calling them back from the hills.

Morven wanted them to go away now that Flint was restored to health, knowing inside, perhaps, that they had stayed here for a reason, and her lover was highly unlikely to do as she requested. They were all together in the restored shack, on seats made from the wood they had found lying around. Ty was good with his hands and had put them together with a facility that argued he could have found a job as a carpenter if he wanted.

'Joe Flint, I think it's time we got out of here.'

He cocked an eye at her, approaching the matter ironically.

'Where would we go?'

'I don't know, probably the nearest town.'

'Then you're mistaken; the three towns are all in the pay

of Ramirez. If we go there we'll stand out like wild geese on a duck pond. They'll pass on the message and we'll be taken back to the fort if we surrender. Or there'll be a bloody battle in the street and we'll die there and then. Either way, we won't be getting out of this by going to town.'

'There are other places.'

'Yep, and if we go anywhere near those we've a huge distance to travel. I don't think we could make it with our limited supplies.'

'I can see what this is working up to,' said Ty.

'What?' asked Flint.

'You're going to do what you came for, ain't you?'

'What does that mean?' asked Matt.

'Well, what did this young idjit come here for?' asked Ty.

'Gold? He still wants the gold?'

'I don't see the point of arguing,' Flint spread out his hands. 'I know where the treasure is housed. The treasure is not at the fort, because Ramirez is not stupid, but at another location that we passed on the way here, one of the old cliff-dwellings of the ancients.'

'Joe, I heard those rumours,' Morven gave him a fierce glare. 'But that area's guarded, there's a lookout on duty all the time. If you went there he would sound the alarm and we'd all be caught.'

'Who says you're going along?'

The girl shook her head fiercely. 'If you're going so am I, that's all there is to it, Joe.'

'I suppose I should be glad that you're so loyal, but sometimes you just invite danger.'

'And you don't? Who's going there in the first place?'

'Whoah! Much as I hate to interrupt a tiff between two lovers,' Ty gave a gentle chuckle, 'you ain't addressed the point, Flint. How do you take out the lookout? He gets on that horn our backside'll be covered in bandits faster than it takes to ride from here to the mine.'

'I suppose we could shoot him out,' said Flint thoughtfully. 'You're the best shot, Ty. Could you conceal yourself behind one of the peaks and take him out from a distance?'

'I guess I could.'

'The only trouble is, you would need to be pretty distant and the guns we managed to bring with us aren't all that good at that range. You would need to get him first time.'

'I guess so.' Ty thought about the matter for a minute, then shook his head. 'Sorry, I couldn't guarantee the shot.'

'Listen to you,' burst out Morven, 'talking this nonsense seriously.'

'Nothing's gonna work,' said Matt, shaking his head, 'nothing.'

'What did we come here for?' said Flint.

'Gold,' said Ty and Matt together. They stared at each other.

'We're not giving up,' said Flint, then a slow smile spread across his face.

'What is it?' demanded Morven.

'I have an idea,' he said.

It was twilight on the second day after the bandits had arrived from the surrounding territories. As was her usual practice Justine went for a walk at night. The fort was a very different place from what it had been just a few days before. The corral was full to bursting and some of the horses had to be housed outside the walls. The camping area behind the bunkhouses, once so sparsely populated, was bursting with the tents that housed many of the new arrivals. They numbered so many that the cookhouse was kept busy making bread and meals day and night. The beer was beginning to run out, and mules from town were making their way up to the fort every day, carrying the necessities for such a large population.

Even though it was starting to get dark and she was surrounded by men, many of whom had been killers of women and children, Justine did not feel any fear. They had all seen her by the side of Ramirez and knew what would happen to them if she was harmed. Besides, she did not stay within the boundaries of the fort for long, slipping through one of the gaps in the wall and taking her walk outside, where she could smell the wild plants and listen to sounds of nature. She exchanged greetings with one of the guards keeping a watchful eye on the boundaries before strolling around the perimeter. When she had gone a further hundred yards she was startled to hear a voice, soft but clear in the semi-darkness, calling her name.

'Justine.'

'Who is it?' She kept her own voice soft and low, a habit she had got into when dealing with Ramirez. Truth to tell, she recognized who it was and found that she was already trembling.

'Don't say any more, just come over here.'

The voice had come from a rocky area near the side of the fort, where low, scrubby bushes grewnear a dip in the ground. She went over to the shadowy form that stood there. He put his finger to her lips and led her away from the walls before daring to turn and speak to her in a low voice.

'Justine, I'm so glad to see you again.'

'I thought you were dead.' She could not help herself, but wrapped her arms around him and held him tight. He responded warmly and the two of them stood there for a while until he gently disengaged himself.

'Justine, I came here for a reason.'

'To see me, especially?'

'Yep, to see you, but not because of what you think. I'm not going to lie with you. I came to this place to get a better future; now that future hangs on you.'

'I was so sad when I thought you were dead, that they had sealed you in there. To find you here like this. . . '

'Shhh.' He put two fingers to her lips. 'I don't understand why you don't leave him. Will you help me?'

'You are going to rob him?'

'I promise, very little will be taken compared to what he has. Little for him, a lot for me. You will save me?'

'To be with her?'

'That's right.'

There was a moment, as Justine stood in the twilight with only her pale features visible, when it might have gone either way. She could have shouted to the guards and ended his time there and then. There would be no more bear-baiting if he was caught now. He would simply be killed. Then she relaxed, although she still did not smile.

'Very well, you have come this far, I owe you. Tell me what I have to do.'

The next day the lookout at the Point overlooking the old citadel in the hill was startled to see Justine arriving alone on her mount. It was still early in the day and he had not long arrived there himself. He supposed she was just out for her usual morning ride, and thought little of the matter as he heard her horse near the base of the mesa on which he stood. He was expecting see her further on towards the blue hills, when he heard a cry of pain and fear.

'Help, I've fallen!'

He cursed and put down his trumpet. If there was one reason for abandoning his post, this was it. In some ways he did not mind, for the days up here were long and boring: except for the excitement of the invaders a few days before, nothing ever happened. He quickly climbed down the rope ladder clinging to the rocky wall before coming to rest on the red soil below. Justine was lying on her side a few yards from the base of the mesa, her horse standing quietly a few feet further on.

'Help, my horse stumbled on a loose stone and threw me.'

'You OK?'

'I'm just a bit winded. If you can help me on to him I'll be able to get back to the fort.'

The man brought her horse over and began to help her to her feet. He could not help thinking it was damn good to hold a woman this pretty in his arms, her scent, her womanly assets, all conspired to distract him as she used him to haul herself to her feet. Suddenly he yelped and let her go, rubbing at his forearm.

'What the hell was that?'

'Big insect, landed and stung you while you were helping me,' she said. The man nodded at this explanation. He made as though about to help her in to the saddle, then he fell to the ground. She had used a rubber bulb and a sharp straw full of the same medicine she gave Ramirez when he could not sleep, to inject into the man. She had given him quite a large dose, but he would survive. He would be out for at least two hours.

The mesa had numerous cracks and small gullies at the base that always remained in shadow. She was young and strong. She dragged the man into one of these, mounted her horse, waved a red bandanna she had brought with her, and then rode back towards the fort.

She had done her bit.

*

Up in the hills, concealed behind some large boulders, Flint saw the signal. He was more than ready to respond. The first thing he did, to the amazement of the others, was go towards the crooked tree and start digging in the ground with a bit of wood he had brought especially for that purpose. He removed a small leather parcel and a couple of weapons he had buried there, then rejoined his party, showing them why he had wasted precious minutes doing this. The leather was wrapped around six sticks of dynamite.

They did not waste time discussing the matter. Instead they tethered their horses on the far side of the hill, looked upwards, and began to climb. What they were looking at was a citadel that had been built hundreds, maybe even thousands of years ago by the Pueblo Indians. The former occupants would have made their way in and out of the buildings and down the sides using rope ladders. The front of the hill at the top was gouged out so that there was an area to stand on, while the entrance to the former dwellings was protected by large rocks that had been painstakingly piled in front, then sealed together by some kind of limestone mortar. It was a difficult place to get to, the climb being made easier by fresh foot- and handholds that had been carved in the soft rock of the hill since the days of the Indians. Ramirez was no fool. He wanted to hide his treasure, but he also wanted to be able to get it out easily enough when he so desired.

They all climbed up together, with Flint in the lead. He was one of those people who seem designed to climb. His recent wound still ached, but he was far ahead of them. His movements were made more urgent by the thought that they were near their goal.

Around the upper half of his body was looped a long rope. Matt carried a net on his own back. The idea was quite simple: they would take what they wanted; lower the treasure to the ground, pack their saddle-bags and go.

This was still on Flint's mind as he stood on the slightly sloping path in front of the former dwelling. He could only marvel at the skills of those who had chosen to live here. This was no plain cavern, but a shaped building carved out of the hill, about twelve feet high and rectangular in shape. There had been a door and four windows but these had all been sealed.

Flint decided to tackle the doorway. The mortar was cracked by exposure to the dry air up here. He managed to place a stick of dynamite in roughly what would have been the four corners of the doorway. By the time he had performed this act the other three had managed to join him. Funnily enough, Matt, with his massive hands, found the handholds extremely hard to use, so he was the last to join them.

'Move back along the ledge,' warned Flint. 'We don't have much time. This will be the crucial moment.' He was right. If the dynamite had become too damp or had not been properly packed, the explosion would be ineffective and they would find themselves in front of an impregnable fortress, which would not only mean that all their efforts had been wasted but also that they put themselves in a dangerous position. for nothing.

He lit each stick in turn, then hastily moved to join the others, who had retreated to the furthest corner of the ledge. They had expected the explosion to be loud, but strangely enough the noise they heard was a huge crump!

This seemed not all that loud but it exerted a lot of pressure on the inner ear. As the dynamite exploded there was a huge outpouring of dust and debris from the entrance to the building. If the guard had still been in place the horn would have been blown by now. As it was, they could only pray that the sound had not travelled across the mesa to where the fort lay.

Flint did not wait too long before moving forward to see what kind of damage had been done. He was pleased to find that the resulting gap was more than big enough for them to get inside the building. They had brought one of the torches from the mine with them. He lit this, then, as the unofficial leader of their small party, he stepped inside, with the two men and the woman following with some caution.

All he could think in the seconds that followed was that the men who had tried to come here earlier had been right to carry out their pursuit. The interior was packed with gold bullion and similar bars made of silver, while wooden cases contained various valuable artefacts such as golden coins, necklaces made of pearls and diamonds, and rings with rubies and diamonds set into them. One box even contained rolled-up paintings, although Flint had no idea what value these works could have.

They wasted no time. As he had indicated to Justine, Flint had no desire to steal all of this treasure. Even one tenth of this could keep them in luxury for the rest of their lives, and he did not want even a tenth; a fortieth would be all that they could carry and that was more than enough for them all.

'It's real,' said Ty, with some astonishment. 'Ya did it, kid.'

Flint could not help laughing at the look of astonishment

on his face. Matt just looked around in mute wonder for a few seconds.

'Brogan was right,' he murmured under his breath.

'Hadn't we better get on with it?' asked Morven, most practical of them all.

Flint set up the net on the ledge and took out some gold bars. Bullion would be the best thing to carry because it could be carried quite easily stowed away in their saddle-bags until they could get to some kind of civilization. The other fact was that the gold could be reburied in a location only they knew of, and where they could get it again safely on some future date.

'Stop,' he said at last when they had loaded the required amount.

'Is that it?' asked Matt, looking more than a little disappointed.

'Yep. Now we don't have time to mess about.'

'Wait a minute, what's that?' asked Morven, pointing in the direction of the fort. Their view was blocked by the small mesa in front of them, but they could hear an ominous sound that came closer and closer as they stood there – the thundering of horses' hoofs. Not just a few horses either, but many of them. Flint reacted by pulling the gold back into the building, helped by the other two men. He also pulled in Morven, who showed a distressing tendency to stay where she was, then he threw his body flat and moved towards the edge.

Below them milled Ramirez and his bandits, along with the other chiefs and men who had promised loyalty to them. They were pointing up the steep sides and shouting, having seen the hole in the place where Ramirez had stored his treasure. Some were dismounting along with Ramirez, ready to come up.

They were trapped. They could fight and die or wait and die anyway.

They had no choice.

CHAPTER SIXTEEN

Justine had found Ramirez confident that his men were on his side. He had been holding a conference with the leaders of the men when she returned from disarming the lookout. She had not killed anybody for Flint, so her conscience was safe and she knew that Flint would take as little of the treasure as he had promised. When she walked into the planning room of the big house her appearance was greeted with a few appreciative chuckles and comments by the men. The air was thick with smoke from cigars and cigarettes. Ramirez gave her a stern look.

'Come back later, woman, this is men's business.'

'Yes, my leader,' she said meekly, before departing. Once outside, though, she listened in to the conversation coming from behind the closed doors. This was not hard to do because the wooden panels were thin and the voices were loud. One of the bandit leaders was vehement in protesting about their work.

'How do we know that you have the gold you speak of? You boast of being able to back this thing, but for you to do that you must have treasure worth millions. Yet you choose this rocky hideout? Do I look like a fool?'

'Then you will find out where I keep my gold and turn on me like dogs,' said Ramirez.

'I swear,' the man who had spoken rounded on the other men, 'let us all swear an oath that such a thing would not be.'

Justine shuddered as they all swore an oath of fealty to Ramirez, for she knew what was coming next. She could also picture his black eyes glittering as he leaned over the oak table at which they sat.

'Listen to me. What you are about to see is nothing. When we control the territory we control vast resources, all there for our taking. Come, we will ride.'

The riders were soon pouring out of the old fort. Ramirez wore his mask to protect his skin from the sun even though it was not yet noon. As they rode towards the Point they did not hear the warning horn, but they heard the sound of the explosion as the dynamite went off. Ramirez cruelly spurred his horse on, riding hard to get to the bottom of the hill where he kept his treasure. From below he could see the gaping black hole that had been blown in the front of the ancient construction. He writhed in anger in the saddle. This was not what he had expected. But he had his own way into the apparently sealed chamber.

He was not a man to hesitate. He had planned to go inside with some of the leaders and show them his resources, taking some of the treasure to use as initial payment. But instead of climbing the steps he turned to the men behind him.

'Come with me,' he said. 'Just you three.'

Like all hills in this district, this one was pitted and scarred by thousands of years of geological change. He took them towards a fold in the hill – then all four men disappeared. It was like a conjuring trick.

At the same time there was a noise from the rear of the horsemen who milled around the base of the retreat. It was the sound of a horn being blown. Most of the men were armed – this was their trade, after all, so they were ready for whatever might happen out here in the hills. They heeled their horses around to face where the noise came from, forgetting about their leaders for that moment.

New riders appeared; soldiers wearing beige, wide-brimmed hats, dark-blue jackets and trousers of lighter blue that were a familiar sight to all Ramirez's men. The new arrivals were carrying army pistols and Remington rifles. They also had swords sheathed at their sides. At their head was a wild-eyed man whom none of the bandits recognized. He was dressed in plain clothes. He carried a gun, too, and behaved like some kind of leader despite his seeming lack of rank. Along with the soldiers he joined the battle in earnest, shooting with the best of them.

Up on the ledge Flint looked down at the arrival of the soldiers. They were such an unexpected sight, bringing some hope to his heart that he could only watch their advance with awe. Why would they be here at all, given the lawlessness of this district and the lack of anyone who was willing to cooperate with the authorities?

Then he saw who was leading them, recognizing the man even from this height. It was Edwardes, the leader of the mining community the bandits had broken up, where Flint had been living for the past week. He was too high to see the man's expression, but Edwardes's determination to crush the bandits who had caused the destruction of his community was evident in every line of his body.

The charge was ferocious, shots being fired immediately the bandits were visible to the soldiers. It was not often that the army was able to descend on such a nest of vipers all gathered in one place, and they were making full use of the opportunity.

Even as Flint watched many of the bandits were shot off their horses and trampled to the very dust, their awful screams cut off as the hoofs of their horses completed the work of the soldiers. The reports of the gunshots were absorbed by the surrounding terrain, so that they sounded like harmless firecrackers going off. But the results were far from harmless, as at least a dozen men died in front of his eyes with gaping wounds to their chests or heads.

'Surrender!' screamed Edwardes, 'Or you will all die!'

But by that time the troops had aroused the ire of the bandits, who responded in kind, firing at will. At least half a dozen blue-clad soldiers went down. The riderless horses of those who had been killed only added to the confusion by milling around and getting in the way of those who would have fought with each other.

It was clear by now that the soldiers were equal to or greater in numbers than the men they were after. The bandit force suddenly lost a lot of will when it came to joining battle. They could not get back to the fort, so they turned their horses and fled into the hills with the army riding after them. It was a complete rout. As they turned and rode off, many more were felled by shots from the army rifles. Those in the army who had run out of bullets took out their swords and spurred their mounts onwards, catching up with those at the rear and cutting them down with a broad sweep that lopped off heads or limbs and caused many more casualties.

Some of the bandits turned round and fired back at the pursuers, wounding and killing more soldiers. Edwardes, who was still in the lead seemed like an implacable demon since, even though others fell around him, with his fixed jaw and that glittering look in his eyes as he shot down more bandits than anyone, he was proof that fortune does indeed favour the brave.

As the soldiers left the valley below in hot pursuit of those who had survived Flint, looking at the retreating criminals, realized that Ramirez was finished. His revolution would come to nothing now.

He moved back so that no one would be able to spot him from below. Not that it would make much difference at the moment because the battle had turned into an affray that would end the time of the men who thought they would be able to start an insurrection that would lead to their ultimate power.

As he came towards the hole he had blown in Ramirez's repository Flint froze where he stood. He could hear the sound of a voice that he knew only too well. Ramirez was inside and he sounded almost insane with rage.

'I weel kill you all, where ees he, the upstart? I will make sure you die now!'

Flint knew that in this situation he did not have much of a chance. He did not have a great deal of weaponry on him. He had had none when they fled from the fortress, so that he'd had to borrow one of Ty's Colt .44s. It was a good gun, the handle worn smooth with many years of use.

A thought occurred to Flint, that perhaps their escape from the fort had not been as much a matter of chance as he had thought. Perhaps Ty was a lot more experienced at this kind of thing than he pretended. He dismissed the thought from his mind as he considered what to do. Then he simply acted as his instincts told him, flattening his body against the wall before turning in through the doorway with his gun at the ready.

As he had expected Ramirez was holding up his three companions; they stood facing him across the treasure chamber. That alone would have been bad enough, but they were also being held up by another three armed brigands, men who looked as if they would be quite happy to die for spoils like these.

'Ramirez!' shouted Flint, his voice reverberating in the confined space. All the weapons turned on him but Flint responded by shooting at the leader, who dodged back but yelled and dropped his gun as the bullet grazed his wrist.

Matt, who saw that all eyes were off him, now used his chance to do what he did best – get up close and personal, throwing haymaker punches that would have felled a horse let alone the two men who were their recipients, one after the other. One of the men staggered backwards and fell into the other, his gun going off, with the bullet ricocheting off the ground. Morven, who had been standing beside Ty, gave a soft groan, but no one paid any attention to that at the moment.

The last man trained his gun on the boxer who had felled his companions. He was about to shoot Matt in the head at point-blank range when Ty drew out the companion of the weapon held by Flint and pumped three bullets into the man. The gun fell out of his hands as the man gave a wordless groan and fell to the ground, already dead. Ty did not waste any time but pumped lead into the other two fallen bandits. They would never rise again. His gun gave a few useless clicks, it was empty.

In the meantime Flint found himself driven backwards by Ramirez. He had lifted his Colt to shoot the leader full in the face, but he too was met by a series of useless clicks. He threw the gun aside and found that they were now meeting on the ledge in front of the ancient Indian construction. Ramirez had seemed to be without a weapon, but now he drew out the silver dagger with a handle shaped like a skull.

The mask that he had been wearing to protect his face from the sun had fallen off during his exertions and the skin of his face was now breaking out, seeming to boil in the direct light. Flint could see the sores erupting on his forehead, face and neck, blood and pus pouring down his contorted features.

'You are to die,' he said, slashing out and forcing Flint backwards. This was a dangerous position to be in. If Flint went right back he would be pressed against the rough stone, with nowhere to go on one side and a drop that would kill him on the other. The knife flashed out, and Flint twisted from one side to the other as it slashed his arm, his leg and his side. He hardly felt the wounding at the time, so sharp was the blade. None of the cuts had been that deep because he had managed to dodge the main thrust of the blade so well, but if this went on he would suffer death by a thousand cuts: not an attractive thought.

In desperation he did something he would never usually have considered. He turned, bent down and pushed his body off the ledge, holding on just by his fingertips. Ramirez had thrown himself forward to lunge at Flint, so that when the latter vanished Ramirez staggered on for a few paces. Flint pulled his body up from the ledge, his fingers bloodied and torn from their contact with the stone, so that he was now behind the one-time leader.

Before Ramirez had a chance to turn around Flint kicked him in the spine, the one place where he knew a blow could badly disable a man. Ramirez gave a roar of pain and anguish, yet still managed to turn. He was within a few feet of Flint now and lifted his arm to throw the ultra-sharp knife. He had one of the most accurate aims Flint had ever seen. Within a second Flint would have a knife embedded between his eyes and there was nothing he could do about it.

As if by some magic spell the weapon Ramirez held with such confidence suddenly dropped from his hand, then clattered to the stony ground. The blow to his spine had travelled along his nervous system and disabled his hand. Flint swiftly picked up the knife and threw it more by instinct than with conscious aim. There was an audible thud as the knife became embedded in the middle of Ramirez's chest. He looked down and saw that the skull on the handle was grinning up at him now, as if in mocking triumph.

'You . . . win,' said the leader hoarsely, then he fell sideways off the ledge.

Some of the rocks below were jagged enough to cause a great deal of damage if you fell from this height. Flint looked over and saw the bloodied remains of the leader sprawled in an unnatural position like a shattered marionette. All his bones must have been broken.

Flint discovered that he himself had not come away from the fight undamaged. One leg of his trousers was soaking with blood from a wound on the upper part of the thigh. Another wound on his side was seeping blood into his jacket. A third wound on his shoulder was weeping steadily.

He staggered into the chamber containing all the gold.

'Where the hell were you?' he asked of his companions. Then he saw that Matt was cradling Morven in his arms and that she too had a wound on her upper body that vented her life blood.

'Flint,' she said weakly, 'Flint.'

'You'll be all right,' he said, coming swiftly to her side, 'just rest where you are, we'll help you.'

'Did you get him?' she asked, her dark liquid eyes fixed on him.

'Yes, I did,' he said. 'He's gone for good now, stabbed to the heart.'

'Thank you, Flint,' said the girl, giving a gasp. She suddenly relaxed in Matt's arms as the final breath left her, and died with her eyes still open, gazing lifelessly at the man who had helped her to achieve her goal. Flint reached out, and with tenderness that he had shown to no man he closed her eyes. Then he stood up and said nothing for what seemed like a lifetime. Matt continued to cradle her, bawling like a baby, unafraid to show his emotions.

'You're wounded,' said Ty, who had seen the whole thing. 'Come on, we'll fix you up.'

After his wounds were bandaged using the materials to hand Flint could not bear to be in that place much longer. He explored the chamber and found that it went back into the hill, leading to other openings linked by wide doorways. It was through one of these that he found what he was looking for. A winding stairwell had been carved into the middle of the hill, leading down to the outside world. It was just wide enough for one person at a time, but even so was a remarkable feat of engineering.

This was Ramirez's secret weapon. It was a way for him to gain access to his gold quickly without anyone else knowing how he performed his trick. It was also why he had a guard on this hill all the time, in case anyone should stumble on the secret entrance by accident.

Flint also found all the tools that Ramirez could ever have needed inside the same chamber that held the stairwell: shovels and picks that had obviously been used in its construction. They took the girl outside and buried her in the shadow of a gnarled tree. Ty held his hat to his chest and gave a short homily to her while the other two looked on. Then they went back up to the treasure.

'I wish I'd never bothered,' said Flint at last, looking at the glittering prizes in disgust.

'Don't be too hard on yourself,' said Ty. 'You never brought her here. She was the one who wanted to avenge her father.'

'We're going to be rich,' said Matt, but with an edge of sadness.

'I wouldn't be too sure of that, son,' said Ty.

They both looked at him in astonishment.

'Let me introduce myself. I'm Tyler Landis, US marshal, sworn to track down this here treasure. Them bandits were never going to take over the territory despite what Ramirez thought. This gold you're looking at belongs to the US Government and has to be returned. I am commandeering this spot for the government right now.'

'So all this has been for nothing,' said Flint. 'Well, I don't want it anyway.'

'Wait a minute,' said Ty, 'look at this other stuff. There's no one around to claim these here coins an' gewgaws, an' I guess if you two boys wanted to help make this place secure you could load up with as much of this stuff as you can before you do so.' He looked at them with a bland expression.

Despite the joylessness of the occasion they swiftly obeyed, because who knew when the government troops would return, arresting everybody? They loaded up their saddlebags with gold coins, diamond rings, pearl necklaces and other objects that would never be traced to their original owners but could be resold for a high price. Then they assisted Ty to make the premises secure.

They were in the shadow of the hill now. It was past midday and they could hear the sound of many horses in the distance.

'You boys go,' said Ty. 'I'll deal with these ones.' He shook hands with them both, and gave a rare, wide grin. 'Sure has been interesting, I'll miss you boys.'

Flint and Matt rode away without looking back.

'I need to go to the fort,' said Flint. They found the gates wide. The fort was empty now except for a few of the older servants and one of the cooks. Obviously everyone had fled when they realized there was a battle going on.

'Oh well,' said Flint, 'at least I tried.'

They rode down the trail, heading for the three towns, discussing their cover story so that if they were questioned at least they would be able to account for their movements.

Then they heard the sound of hoofs behind them. Flint turned, gun already in hand, only to see Justine catching up with them.

'I was looking for you,' she said.

'Well, you found me,' said Flint.

The three of them rode on together.